Love is a Four Letter Word

ZARA STONELEY

Harper*Impulse* an imprint of
HarperCollins*Publishers Ltd*
77–85 Fulham Palace Road
Hammersmith, London W6 8JB

www.harpercollins.co.uk

A Paperback Original 2014

First published in Great Britain in ebook format by HarperImpulse 2013

A catalogue record for this book
is available from the British Library

ISBN: 978-0-00-759179-4

Automatically produced by Atomik ePublisher from Easypress

ZARA STONELEY

I've been writing stories for just about as long as I've been reading them – it's rumoured that I'm related to Elizabeth Gaskell, so maybe it's in the genes!

I live in a country cottage in the UK with a naughty mouse catching, curtain climbing cat, my wonderful guitar playing, video making, Minecraft mad teenage son and a wine drinking, sun loving, master chef in the making, sexy alpha hero.

I love my family, sexy high heels, sunshine, wine, good food, cats, horses, dogs, music, coffee, writing and reading - but not necessarily in that order! And I like my heroes just how I like my coffee – hot, strong and moreish.

You can find more about me, and all my contact details at www.zarastoneley.com. Please stop by – I love to meet new people.

To the man in my life – who knows that being a little bit bad can be good...

Chapter One

"Which bit of *no* don't you understand?"

"From my side of the table it looked pretty much like a yes, darling. Come on, admit it, you want it."

"If I wanted *it* I'd ask, okay?"

"Oh, you were asking, babe."

Georgie cringed. She was nobody's babe; he'd been watching the wrong type of films. She crossed her arms across her chest and tried to stare him down, but from the glassy look in his eyes he was too inebriated to register anything, let alone a put down, unless it involved a minor act of violence. "I was just being polite."

Surprisingly strong fingers gripped her arm before she had a chance to move further away, digging into the bare skin, leeching the colour away. The gasp had to be her, but being manhandled wasn't on any wish list she'd ever had. Well, not like this. And it hurt.

"Hey, let go." She was drunk, but obviously not as drunk as he was, because when she pulled away he staggered.

"There's a word for girls like you."

Georgina Hampton took a step back and turned away. "And there's more than one word for dicks like you." She was glad she'd only muttered it under her breath, because when she glanced back over her shoulder, he looked like he wasn't about to give up.

Yeah, she'd been friendly, even flirted a bit. But that was her job. And since when was there a rule that said if you had a laugh with a guy he was entitled to get into your knickers?

As Georgie pushed open the door that separated the loud, claustrophobic heat of the club from the real world a sudden wave of exhaustion swept over her. It had been a long day, she'd had one too many vodka shots, and unwanted male attention was the last straw. She concentrated on keeping her high heels both going in the same direction as she headed for the door, not sure if it was tiredness or drink that was playing havoc most with her balance. One thing she did know was that every step was another one closer to home and her bed.

"Off early, can't stand the pace?" One of the bouncers grinned at her, he knew that exiting at this time wasn't her normal form, and as he swung the outside door open the rush of cool night air almost knocked her off balance. "You okay?" He was giving her a weird look.

"Yeah." She tried a grin. "Had a shitty day, that's all." She didn't know his name and he didn't know hers, but she was at the club often enough for the professional distance to have dropped, just a bit.

"Hey, stop." The drunken idiot had followed her all the way to the door. "Georgie, I said stop."

"You sure you don't need a hand, love?"

She shook her head at the bouncer. She didn't want trouble. Not again. Carol would have a fit, a major prima donna explosion if there was even a hint of a bad smell this week. What was it with step-mothers that thought just because they had your dad under the thumb then they had the right to ruin your life as well?

"I'm fine, thanks." She took a step out onto the pavement and almost instantly regretted turning the offer down, as Sebastian, 'but you can call me Seb', sent a wave of alcohol drenched breath down her neck. Good job she didn't feel queasy or that really would tip the balance.

Yes, she knew his name. But that was the absolute limit of the relationship. Which sadly he didn't get. He'd been one of a group of guys, rich guys, who had rolled into the restaurant that night where she was front of house. He'd flirted, and she'd done what she did best back. Avoided his hands, but caressed his ego. It was her job, and she was damned good at it. Trouble was, the stupid twat had presumed the service extended after hours and he'd followed her to the club that the staff had headed to when the restaurant had closed.

His hand was on her waist and she felt like retching, and her heart had hitched up a beat. She'd had him down as wet, but even a complete drip was strong when they were fuelled with beer and chasers. Stronger than her.

"Get your hands off me." She fought to keep her voice even and low. Gritting her teeth helped.

"Didn't I tip well enough darling? I thought it would be plenty for a girl like you."

"Fuck off, okay. Is that clear enough?"

"Or what?"

Shit, with his arm still clamped around her waist he'd somehow managed to propel her past the frontage of the club, to the edge of the deserted car park and suddenly it hit her. *Or what?* Damned good question.

His clammy hand had tightened around her, the damp warmth seeping through the thin fabric as though it was skin on skin. She was going to be sick. A mix of shots tumbled around in her stomach, hit the bubbles of Prosecco, and mingled with the slightest trace of fear. She swallowed down the tang of bile.

"Just get your hands off me, okay? I'm not your type."

"Let me be the judge of that, gorgeous." She would have liked to have slapped that leery smirk right off his face, but keeping her balance in the killer heels and working out whether to knee him in the groin, stamp on his toes or ditch the stilettos and run was priority at the moment.

He pushed her a step back, further into the dark shadows that draped the side of the building. Then his hand closed round her wrist. A band of iron, fingertips digging into her skin as she pulled back, burning. He snorted and the mix of beer fumes and stale cigarette filled her lungs as he leaned in closer. Close enough to kiss. Close enough to make the knot in her stomach pull just a bit tighter, and her heart pound like it was about to burst free.

Think, Georgie, think. She turned her head away as his other hand came up, at the side of her, against the wall, blocking her escape. Not that escape was on the agenda until she managed to drag her wrist free from his grasp. He swayed closer and even with a sideways glance she could see his gaze was fixed on her mouth. If she stayed here a second longer it would be too late. She twisted, bent down, dodged under the arm that held hers, hoping he'd loosen his grip so she could break free, but instead as she ducked he did the one thing she hadn't expected. Twisted her arm up behind her back. Pressed her cheek hard against the damp, darkness of the wall, until sharp splinters of brick bit into her skin. Georgie shut her eyes.

"Oh, so that's how you want it is it. Kinky one, eh?" The heat of his breath was fanning her neck, his heavy, suffocating body close against hers, and she was grimly aware of his rock hard erection, pressed against her. "Like it from behind do you?"

Fuck. She had to get away. She just had to. Being groped against a wall was so not how her life was supposed to be working out. She took a breath, opened her eyes, and then kicked back with all her strength, raking her heel down his shin, stamping down hard on his foot for good measure as he loosened his grip slightly. All she had to do was get his hands off her. He was pissed, he wouldn't be able to run after her.

"Bitch. Christ, what the fuck was that for?" He reached instinctively for his leg with one hand, but it still hurt like hell as she pulled back, dragged her arm from his grasp, feeling the burn of friction, his skin against hers.

There were a whole shopping list of things she could have answered with, but she didn't trust herself to say a word. Keeping her mouth shut was safer for more reasons than one.

Georgie staggered back, one step, another, turned to run.

"You got a problem?" The deep drawl stopped her short, and she could have sworn literally stopped her heart for a beat.

"A problem? She's fuckin' psycho that one, you're welcome to her." She hardly felt Seb push his way past her, was only dimly aware of the scatter of stones as he staggered back towards the road, finding a new swear word with each step he took across the rough parking lot.

"I said, are you okay?" There was a guy, and he was staring at her, like she was stupid. She stared back, because she couldn't not. Dark curls, green eyes, a dimple in the middle of his chin, a stud in his ear. Black motorbike leathers.

Georgie swallowed, cleared her tight, dry throat. Wow. The dark knight. In a parking lot in Cheshire. Stared a bit more. Whatever they were serving in there was stronger than she'd thought. "Sure. Erm, no problem." Well, only one. Him. And he was the kind of problem she liked. She hoped she wasn't licking her lips, but she probably was. "I'm fine." *Once I remember how to breath normally again. And work out if I'm hallucinating or not.*

She took another steadying breath, to replace the oxygen she'd lost while she'd been holding her breath. This wasn't a weak chinned, clammy handed type of idiot like Seb. The type who slobbered over you and pawed. Oh, no. This guy was trouble, with a capital T. Otherwise translated as yum, with a capital Y.

"Good. I'll leave you to it then."

"No."

He slanted his head slightly, probably because she'd shouted it out like a weirdo.

"Don't go. I mean, hang around for a bit, will you?" It could have been a residue of adrenalin from being pinned against that wall, but whatever it was her heart was hammering and her body had this strange buzz resonating through it, and she was pretty damned sure it had nothing to do with fear.

He chuckled and the sound fingered its way down her spine. "I don't think he'll be rushing back for seconds. So, are you?"

"Am I what?"

"Psycho."

"I'll let you decide that." She took a step closer to him, which just about took her to the spot where she could smell the mix of spice, wood and musk. Earthy. Nice. "Not that it would bother you, I'm sure."

"Are you now?" He let her close that gulf of ten inches between them, let her reach out to rest a finger on the top of the zip of his leather jacket. Cold metal against warm, the tang of leather and oil layered over the tantalising scent of pure male.

"Very sure. Can I see your bike?"

He looked faintly amused, but from the way his stance had widened and those gorgeous eyes had darkened she knew she had him. Hers for the taking. But he'd kept his hands jammed in his pockets, like he was determined to make her do all the running.

"And there I was thinking it was me you were interested in."

"I am. You and the bike, together."

"You'll have to promise not to rake those heels down the tank."

It was then that she recognised him. It was the way he said it, that ever so slight judgemental edge to his voice. Jake Harcourt. He'd been like that when he was cocky sixteen. Daring, in control. Leader of the pack. And she'd been the podgy teenage girl in her carefully ironed blouse and spotless flat shoes. If she'd not had a drink or five maybe she'd have clicked earlier, maybe not. It was a lifetime ago. And he wasn't a lanky tearaway teenager now. He was a man. Boy, had he grown into a man.

Back then was another time, of schoolgirl crushes, of secret Valentine's cards being pushed into lockers, of wanting the rough tough poster boys and knowing it was a step too far. Then. Bad had been plain bad back then, now it was good.

"I won't leave a scratch. I promise."

He raised an eyebrow and just like that he'd gone from a little bit naughty to full on bad, and Georgie felt her throat dry as the anticipation swirled into a knot of excitement in her stomach.

"No scratches at all?"

The smile twitched at her mouth. "Well, not from the heels. And not on the tank." She rested the very tips of her nails on his jawbone, let them drag across the rough stubble until they rested under his chin, then she leant in, let her breasts rub against the smooth hide of his jacket, closed her teeth around the fullness of his lower lip and pulled back just far enough so that she could glance up, see the look in his eye.

Jake met the coy look she shot through those long eyelashes and wondered if his luck was in or he'd just gone stark staring mad. He'd kicked up the motorbike from pure frustration, barely paused to grab his helmet, and then gunned into the centre of town looking for something, but not knowing what.

Maybe he'd found it.

He'd skidded into this car park because it was quiet. The lull before the 2am outpouring of drunken bodies. And for a brief moment he'd thought about parking up and getting slaughtered before hitching a lift back home. Until he'd heard the voices, and the girl with the cut glass tone had done her best to out-stride her toff of a boyfriend.

For a second he'd thought she was in trouble, which was why, against his natural inclination, he'd stuck his nose in. But she'd handled it, despite the fact that even in the dark he could tell the colour had leached from her face, he could smell the fear, hear the tightness in her words. When you'd got into tight spots like he had, you developed a second sense that told you if you were going to win or lose even before the trouble started.

But after a few seconds of staring at him like he was the man from Mars she'd recovered. Which was as fast a recovery as he'd seen in a long time. Now she was looking at him like he was a prime cut, and it seemed as good a way to burn off his anger as any. He recognised the adrenalin rush, a dance with danger that could send you high before you fell back down. She was ready to ride that wave, ready for the next challenge, and he was just lucky enough to be the one nearest. He wasn't kidding himself that it was anything more than that. Tomorrow she might wonder what the fuck had got into her, but tonight…

Her cool, elegant fingers were on his chin sending an urgent shiver of a message to his already tingling groin, then she leant in and nipped his lip with sharp teeth. Any more of that and he'd be groaning like a randy teenager. He pulled back, half turned in the direction of his bike and her gaze followed his line of sight.

"Can I have a ride?" She dropped the seduction routine, and her hands, like a switch had been flicked.

"What kind of ride did you have in mind?"

Those dark brown eyes were gleaming. He knew her type, used to getting what they wanted, when they wanted. And right now, if she wanted him it wasn't a problem. She wanted the fast ride, the rough and tumble. The danger, the explosion. Then she'd walk away. Perfect. For both of them.

She stared at the motorbike, forgot about teasing his lips and headed straight for the machine. "Fast. I want to go fast." She broke her pace briefly to throw the words over her shoulder and then she was there. Running the ruby red talons over the black paintwork.

He'd not had a pillion rider for a long time. He'd never had one with a dress so short it barely needed hitching up, legs that long and heels that high. So, they weren't going far, whatever she had in mind. Now wasn't the time.

"You're not exactly dressed for a ride."

She chuckled, and he hadn't been expecting a sexy low vibration like that.

"It's my work gear." She grinned, for the first time, and through the mask of a sexy siren slipped a mischievous girl out to have fun, which made up his mind. He wanted her. Now.

"Some job."

"I'm front of house at The Veneto."

Which explained a lot of things, including the groper. Including the confidence. Jake had never been in The Veneto, it was the type of place he'd cross the road to avoid. A top end restaurant, full of the rich and famous, swilling away their fortunes on expensive wine and eating their way through enough carbs and fat to fuel an army of people who actually did something with their lives.

He let his gaze drift over her lazily again. A black sheath dress that fitted where it touched, caressing every curve of her toned body. It was modest at the neck, but dropped low at the back and where it sat high on her thighs it was just crying out to be nudged that inch or two further. There wasn't much left to the imagination, but enough. Enough to make him desperate to go there. Explore. She didn't need the extra height of the heels, and although he'd never have called himself a leg man this pair were doing something to his body that they shouldn't.

And running his hands up from her indecent shoes, all the way up those silk covered calves to the soft, warm flesh he knew he'd find under her skirt was something he wanted to do. Now.

"Sure you don't want to go back and make up with the toff?"

"You're funny." She'd straddled the bike, slid her hands along the tank until she was stretched out on the machine then smiled at him. "People like that bore the pants off me, they haven't a clue how to live. You going to join me and prove you do?"

"I don't need to prove anything." He handed her a helmet. "You know what? You talk too much."

"I know." She smiled. "Why don't you try and make me scream instead?"

"Your wish is my command." He gave a mock bow, then gunned up the engine before either of them could have second thoughts. The rumble threaded through his body and her thighs tightened around his hips as they took off. He could have sworn he could feel the damp heat between her thighs pressed against him, could feel her breasts pressed against his back as she leaned in and her hands snaked around him, slipped down lower between his thighs.

She was light on the back, moving with him as he headed out of the town and took the narrow road that threaded its way up to the forest and, before he'd even decided where they were going, her hands had slipped lower, touching him with a need that matched his mood. He wasn't going far, because for what he had in mind he didn't want to warm the engine up too much, and the way she was messing with his body was already interfering with his mind.

Jake slowed the machine, turned off the road. And she was still when he pulled up, apart from the feather light touch from her fingertips. When he turned she just looked at him, then matched his moves as he undid his helmet and dropped it to the ground. He stepped slowly off the bike, leaving it on the stand, engine ticking over.

Georgie froze astride the bike, feeling vulnerable as he stepped off, not quite sure what was going to happen next, but knowing that the air that had been whistling around her, the heat of him between her legs and the gentle, almost unbearable throb of the engine was turning her into a quivering mass of need.

"Now you, darling, are going in the driving seat, but don't presume for one moment you're in control." His voice was soft against her ear, the warmth of his breath fanning out over her cheek as he lifted her forward onto the seat that was still warm from his body. "Lean forward, hold the handlebars." She stretched forward, the heat and tremble of the engine teasing nipples that were already hard, tormenting her swollen clit as his hand rested in the small of her back, pressing her closer to the machine. She could feel it already starting, the slow relentless climb of an orgasm, the rolling need radiating out from her centre.

He kept one smouldering hand resting on her for a moment, then turned his full attention back to his leathers, cursing as he fought with them. Then he was back on the bike, behind her. "You can rev it up you know." There was humour in the dark soft voice. His hands slipped up her thighs, round her hips, under her dress, his fingers tracing along her knicker line, either side of her mound, his thumbs circling with a pressure that told her he wasn't going to mess. One hand slipped between her legs, traced along her slit until he found her clit and she groaned as he touched her. Whimpered as he increased the pressure, as one finger slipped inside her. "You really do want it don't you?" He lifted her slightly from the seat. "Hold on tight, darling."

She was holding her breath with need, but when he sank inside her she still screamed. Screamed as the weight of his body against her pressed her throbbing clit into the shudder of the bike, screamed as she came with urgent pulses. "Oh. My. God." She could barely get the words out.

He waited, held still as she shuddered around him and then as her body subsided he started. Full long strokes that filled her. Georgie clung onto the handlebars, trying desperately to control the slide of her body against the bike, to control the friction as he gripped her hips with firm fingers and slammed into her. She lifted her head, stared unseeing at the trees that surrounded them, and the animal sounds had to be her as she growled and cursed, writhed against him, as her body fought the vibrations, willed the orgasm to build higher, higher. And then she couldn't hold that moment any longer. She was unfurling inside, her body pulsing more urgently this time, and he seemed to expand inside her as she closed around him. Gripping, wanting, needing, until he swore, pulled her savagely back against him. And then nothing. Silence apart from the sound of their breathing, panting. Dark.

He pulled out. Gently flicked her knickers back into place with one finger. Eased her up with strong hands until she was leaning back against the warmth of his chest and it felt weirdly familiar as he held her. Then he seemed to realise. Slowly dropped his arms away and she could almost feel him setting the distance between them.

"You okay?"

She nodded. Tugged at her lower lip with sharp teeth, because she didn't know what else to do.

And he was off the bike, passed her a helmet wordlessly and they were back on the road heading for the town before she could think of a single thing to say to him. He weaved his way round the edge of town and pulled up outside her home, the old family home that she'd just returned to after years away, without even asking where she needed dropping.

Georgie clambered off the bike. Stood awkwardly on the kerb and he reached out, straightened her dress down. Flipped his visor up.

"Who said I lived here?"

"Who'd have thought sweet little Georgina would turn into such a naughty girl?"

Georgie stared at him. She'd never even thought he knew her name when they were at school, and she'd not been back in town for years. The witch called Carol had made sure of that. She'd sweet talked Alfie into alternating between keeping her in the mouldy mansion in the back of beyond and sending her off to a stuffy boarding school to wear big knickers and starchy shirts. Anywhere that meant they didn't have to do anything, could just ignore her. Georgie refused to think of him as 'Dad' any more, he was Alfie. Carol's conquest. Carol's puppet. Well they couldn't ignore her now she was big enough to say no.

"Is that what they teach you at posh schools these days?"

It was like he'd read her mind. "Better than learning how to balance a book on your head."

"Can you do that too?" He looked grave, serious. Was studying her like he thought he'd made a mistake.

"Not at the same time."

This time he ignored the flippant comment, didn't join in with the banter. "Don't let having it all fuck you up, Georgie girl."

"What's that supposed to mean?"

"There's nothing wrong with nice." Which was even more confusing.

He flicked his visor down, so all she could see was the dark shadow of his eyes.

"Do you want to come in?" She hadn't meant to say it, she never said it. But it just came spilling out.

"No thanks. You got what you wanted, better to leave it at that, eh?" He revved up the bike hard, swung it in a tight circle and she was left standing on the pavement with the smell of exhaust fumes acrid in her nostrils.

Prick. Georgie slammed the door behind her, dropped her purse in the hallway and headed for the kitchen. He'd got what he wanted as well, hadn't he? Wasn't that what it was about? She glanced at the bottles of white wine that lined the fridge, then with a sigh reached for the bottle of water.

It was the way he'd looked at her. A mixture of anger and concern. A bit like the look her father used to give her when she'd been naughty and he'd been asking her why. He was one hundred per cent sober, unlike her, but he'd had this restrained anger about him that made her want to call him back. Ask him why. But she never did that. Never asked. Not any more, not these days.

And he was wrong, whatever he meant. There was a hell of a lot wrong with nice. Being nice, having nice. Nice had left her with a shit life and no-one who gave a monkeys about her. Nice was a one way street.

She tipped what was left of her drink down the sink. At least being bad meant she got something back.

Chapter Two

"What has got into you?" Ella put her feet up on the glass topped coffee table so that they could both admire her new shoes. "Pissing off is one thing, but you never even answered my texts."

Georgie could hear a note of hurt and felt an instant stab of guilt. "I'm sorry. Really sorry." She knew what it felt like to be ignored so she didn't often do it. Well, not to friends. She picked at a loose thread on the cushion she was holding. "He's an ass. An insufferable jerked up ass."

"So you said."

"I'm sorry. But how can he be so fucking sanctimonious about being nice? I mean, since when did he do what he was supposed to?"

"Exactly."

There was a dry edge to her tone and Georgie glanced up sharply. "Meaning?"

"What is it about you and bad boys?"

"You should try it." She felt the grin creep onto her face. "That motorbike—"

"Georgie!"

"Sorry, just saying."

"I mean, if you're doing it for the kicks then fine, I suppose. But you're really doing it to piss off your dad and Carol, aren't you?" She paused. "Aren't you?"

"Can we drop the lecture? I've got a bad enough headache as it is."

Ella sighed. "Fine. So, why did you leave so early?"

"That dick from the restaurant was hassling me, and I was tired."

"The city wanker?"

"That's the one. I wish I'd just poured the contents of the ice bucket over him after he'd paid the bill, they were just so pissed up and loud I'm sure all the other customers would have thanked me."

"At least a guy like that wouldn't use you."

"Just fuck me you mean?"

"You know what I mean, at least you'd know he wanted your body and not your money."

"Ella, I can't believe you just said that. He was a complete slime-ball." She shuddered. "Can you imagine him slobbering and pawing all over you?"

"No, I can't believe I said it really." Ella sighed. "But those down and out guys you keep flirting with just screw you around."

"I like being screwed."

She laughed. "You know what I mean. You pay for everything, they get the high life, then——"

"Then I dump them, if they really try it on." The only time she'd really got burned was with the guy who'd managed to nick her credit card and run up a mega bill before it had even occurred to her that it could be him. And she wasn't falling for that one again. She had thought there was something a bit shifty about him, but the way he'd pinned her to the bed and made her do exactly what he wanted had turned her on something rotten. He'd been rough and he'd talked dirty, telling her just what he was going to do to her. Her body started to liquefy just at the thought. Nice. Well, it had been for a while. Until the novelty had worn off and he'd stuck his grubby fingers in her purse.

"But don't you want a nice guy, one you're not looking for an excuse to dump?"

"No, Ella. Now stop sounding like grumpy old Alfie. When I'm ready to give up on life and settle down with some rich namby-pamby mummy's boy and breed, you'll be the first to know."

"Really?"

"Don't hold your breath though, it could be a one way trip to asphyxiation."

Ella shook her head. "I give up. Are we supposed to be working?"

"Yeah." Georgie picked up the sheet of paper that was on the sofa at the side of her. "Finding a location for this shoot, and a list of models. I mean, what is it about the great outdoors, what's wrong with a nice city shoot?"

"For country stuff?" Ella giggled.

"But it isn't proper country stuff is it? It's country stuff for city people so they can pretend they're having a relaxing time. Not that the country is relaxing. Latte and shoe shopping sounds a much better deal to me."

"Says the country girl."

"Reformed." She stared blankly at the sheet of paper. "And can you honestly think of a male model we've used recently who looks *rugged*? He's even put 'modern day John Wayne' in brackets after it. Good job it's in fucking pencil then I can rub it out, I mean, what the hell does that mean?"

"Rugged." Ella wriggled and settled deeper into the cushions. "A real man, with abs and muscles and… how about your biker boy?"

"Jake? Piss off, I am not asking Jake. Stop looking at me like that. No. No way, and he's not a model."

"But Toby doesn't want a model, he wants a *real* man. A bad boy, and he knows you're the expert."

"Will you stop keeping saying *real* like you're saying alien."

"It would give you a chance to see him again, you know you want to."

"No, I don't. You can't even look me in the face when you say it, wimp."

"Where does he live? Have you got his number?"

"How should I know where he lives? You're sounding like catty

Carol now."

Ella didn't rise to the bait. "You've got a pic? We can flash it around town, we'll soon root him out."

"He's not a fox gone to earth."

"People will know him if he's half as sexy as you say, well the girls will anyway."

"You're beginning to sound like a stalker, and no I haven't got a photo. Was I supposed to shout 'smile' while he was shagging my brains out on a motorbike?" Georgie closed her eyes. Let's face it, he was exactly what Toby was after. A dark, brooding figure in the background. A guy who'd look sexy in torn dirty jeans and a T-shirt in a way that none of the models they could afford would look. *She* didn't want to see him again. He'd given her the orgasm of a lifetime, but hey, how much of that was down to a few drinks and the thrum of the engine? No, she definitely didn't want to see him again. But, if they used him on the shoot he would just be a hired hand. He wouldn't get a chance to wind her up and be rude to her. Not that he'd been outright rude, just courteous in a rude way that got under her skin.

"So, what is it with you and this Jake? Did you snog behind the bike sheds at school or something?"

"No." More's the pity, except I was a dull little mouse back then. "We were at the same school but we might as well have been on different planets." For all the notice he took, except he did remember me, which is a weird one. "He was one of the bad boys and I was one of the good girls."

"Yeah." Ella laughed. "Sure you were."

But she had been. She'd worked hard, been happy. Until her parents had split up, and she'd been shipped off to a crappy boarding school in the back of beyond.

"Okay, maybe I wasn't that good." She forced a grin onto her stiff face. Ella didn't know what her life had been like. Ella only knew the person she'd turned herself into. The girl who knew what she wanted and went out and got it. On her own. With as many thrills and spills crammed in along the way as she could manage. "But Jake was definitely bad. I didn't recognise him at first, it was a long time ago. And he definitely didn't have a big beast like that ready to be unleashed when we were at school."

"You are so rude. So?"

"So, what?"

"Is he the real deal? Are you going to go dig him out so we can all have a look?"

"I don't know." She nibbled the side of her nail.

"I'm sure Toby will sort something out if we can't, I mean he'll understand that you can't always deliver."

Georgie shook her head slowly at Ella. She was winding her up, challenging her because she knew Georgie didn't like to fail. Ever.

Ella raised an eyebrow, sensing victory. "It's your call."

And yeah, he was the real deal. "I'll try and find him, ask him." He'd say no. What was it he'd said? Don't let having it all fuck you up? Something told her that Jake didn't want it all, he never had. He'd always shunned the rich kids at school, kept his distance and kept his pride. And she had a horrible feeling that even flashing her posh frocks and posy job made him angry. He thought she was a rich, spoiled brat who just used people. He hadn't had to say it, it was in his eyes, in that slightly judgemental tone he'd tried not to let creep into his voice. He'd taken her out on his bike because she'd asked, and because he'd wanted her as much as she wanted him. But he didn't want anything else to do with her.

Which could make this tricky. But she wanted to know why. Which made it even trickier. What did she care? He was a thug with a chip on his shoulder. Except he wasn't a thug. Bugger.

She tried not to grin, look like she didn't care either way. "If he says no, then it's your turn to think of someone, Ella."

"If he says no, then you're losing your touch, wild child."

"Thanks."

"Welcome. So where do we start?"

"We?" Georgie raised an eyebrow.

"We." Ella folded her arms. "What does he do?"

"Do?"

"Can we cut the monosyllabic responses George, I know you're smarter than that. What does he do, you know, for a job?"

"How the hell am I supposed to know?"

"So what did you two talk about then?"

"Talk?" She raised the eyebrows as high as they could go and looked at her friend as though she'd sprouted an extra head. "This wasn't supposed to be the start of a beautiful relationship, Ella."

"Sorry, I forgot for a moment there who I was talking to."

Georgie stared at the ceiling. One thing she'd liked about this place when she was growing up was that everyone knew everybody else. And their business. Which she hated now, but… "I know somebody who is good at talking. Mrs Bea. Come on, we're going for a walk."

"Walk?"

Georgie grinned at the way Ella was staring at her feet. Beautifully encased in her new, totally impractical, designer shoes. "Now who can't string a sentence together?" She still wasn't entirely convinced this was a good idea, but the damned man seemed to have taken residence in her head, and the only way to evict him was to see him in broad daylight when she was sober. Then he wouldn't be the bad boy super stud she'd imagined. He'd be normal, boring and not in the slightest bit interesting at all. He probably had a weak chin, and spots. And a bad haircut. And he was probably so rough at the edges he wouldn't even do for the shoot. "Let's go hunt us down a biker boy."

***

The sweet shop wasn't quite how she remembered it. The bell still pinged when you opened the door, but that was about it. Obviously, just selling plain old sweets didn't cut the mustard these days, you needed to sell them labelled as sugared candy or 'Olde Worlde' and replace the pocket money prices with wage packet ones.

And cuddly Mrs Bea had been replaced by a sullen girl with long, straight, blonde hair and a scowl. If she'd been in earlier she'd have known, but somehow since returning to the town sweets hadn't been high on her priority list. Men kept the pounds off the hips, well at least the type she'd been after did, sugar put them on. So she'd concentrated on the boys.

"Wow, look at these George, I've not seen candy necklaces since I was a kid." Ella was dangling a string of sweets from one finger, a wide grin on her face. "Hey, and sherbet dips, and have you seen this they've got gobstoppers."

"Now I know what the expression like a kid in a candy shop really means." Georgie rolled her eyes in what she hoped was a theatrical, and not a sarcastic, fashion. But Ella didn't care, she was too busy skipping from one new delight to the next. Literally.

"Well my, if it isn't little Georgina Hampton. And haven't you grown up?"

Georgie spun round at the sound of the familiar kind but firm tone of Mrs Bea. Her hair was shorter, slightly more curled and the grey that had been creeping in last time they'd met had taken over. But the round face was instantly recognisable, the twinkling eyes surrounded now by a few more wrinkles. And the broad grin was the one she remembered. If Father Christmas had been a woman, he'd have been Mrs Bea.

Beatrice Stone and her sweet shop had been a childhood treat that no amount of hard knocks could make her forget.

"I'd heard you were back in town, dear."

See, she'd been right. That was just typical of this place, everyone over the age of thirty probably knew where she was working, how long she was staying (even though she didn't herself) and who she'd been talking to. And what she'd been doing on a motorbike last night. She felt the colour rise to a glow in her cheeks and felt like some naïve kid who'd been caught out kissing behind the bike sheds. Not that she'd ever actually done that when she was at school.

Mrs Bea chuckled and the temperature went up another notch, if that was possible. She was not, was definitely not, going to let coming back here send her back to her teens. She was stronger than that, she'd changed. She was who she wanted to be.

"So, you're back at the old place then?"

"No, in the apartment." She picked up a lollipop, turned it slowly in her fingers. "I didn't want to stay in the house, it's too big." Not that it was hers to stay in any more. Bea would know, but Bea probably just wanted to know more. She glanced up and the older woman was watching her closely. "And they—" she wasn't going to say the witches name again, "—had rented it out anyway." She shrugged. Carol had been thrilled, almost orgasmic in her ecstasy, if that was possible for a woman her age and mass, when she'd told them she was going back home for the summer. And Alfie had looked totally relieved. He'd passed a half-hearted 'are you sure that's what you want' then hadn't waited for a response. Oh yeah, they couldn't wait to get rid of her and the only fly in the ointment has been the fact that they'd put the house, her home, out on long term rent. But then he'd remembered it had an annexe, and he'd moved heaven and earth to get it cleaned up, decorated and aired for her. Amazing how fast people could move when they really wanted to get rid of somebody. Not that they knew why she was really going back. She'd wondered who the germ of an idea that had been growing in her head would frighten more, if she ever mentioned it, her or Alfie. He'd probably clam up, head her off if he knew. Like he always did when she mentioned anything to do with the past.

"And how are your father and Carol?"

"Fine." She put the lollipop back, and ignored the question on Bea's face. She wasn't going to talk about them. It had been a long overdue parting of the ways, and she would have moved earlier if she'd had the money to do it. But she'd flunked school, so he made her stay on until she had at least some qualifications to her name. And, after that, the first year of her art course had been great, but then Carol had kicked up such a fuss that he'd forced her into some stupid college where she was supposed to learn some 'life skills', yeah how to woo and wed it should have been called, before finally giving up and letting her choose how she wanted to live her own life.

She could almost feel the scowl forming on her face. She hated him for giving in to her step mum and not letting her finish the art course. She'd actually liked that one, but after the incident with the teacher… She sighed inwardly, it wasn't her fault he was hot and wanted a muse, well was it? Artists were like that.

Being stuck in the sticks with boring old Alfie, Carol and their brood of boring kids hadn't been her idea of fun. Working for them in their crap company wasn't what she wanted to do with her life either. Being back here for the summer was marginally better. They didn't want her in their hair, any more than she had the urge to be there. But the stupid old fart had to get the last word in, if she hadn't got a job sorted and a plan for the future by the end of the summer then she had to go back – to 'discuss things'. Well, to hell with them. She'd walked into The Veneto just as the front of house was walking out. It had been perfect timing, fate. And with her upmarket, boarding school background, the polished finish that the stupid college course had given her, and clothes to match the clients, she'd slid into place like she'd been there forever.

And on the second day at work she'd bumped into Ella and her mates doing a shoot at the restaurant. She'd watched them for a while, then tentatively suggested a different, much better spot to take photographs and before she knew it she was unofficial location scout.

So ancient Alfie and catty Carol could take a hike. She'd got two jobs. And that was just the start.

"Fine?" Bea was studying her carefully.

Fine, as long as she could keep the fifty mile gap between her and them. She nodded.

"Well, it's lovely to see you back, dear. I've missed you. Oh my, your friend has got a sweet tooth." She chuckled, and Georgie turned to see Ella depositing an armful of sweets on the counter with a sheepish grin. The sullen blonde had miraculously transformed into the epitome of customer service when Bea had appeared. All smiles and 'how can I help you?'

"They aren't all for me." Ella had realised they were watching her unloading her sugared bounty.

"Sure, I believe you."

"They're for the crew as well. Honest. They will love them."

The crew. She was here for a reason, here because Bea knew everyone and everything that happened in this place.

"Mrs Bea, Bea, I was wondering, you don't know where…"

"Rowena."

"Sorry?"

"He's out at Rowena's place."

Fuck it was worse than she'd thought. Bea probably did know about the bike. And everything that had happened. Oh Christ, she resisted the urge to cover her face with her hands.

"I wondered when you'd get round to asking."

They had to be a coven of witches. They just had to be. All these respectable looking old women must get together around their modern day cauldron, or crystal ball, or whatever and watch what everybody was up to.

"On Marsh Lane."

It took a moment to register. "Marsh Lane?" She stared blankly at the older woman. He couldn't be there. He just couldn't.

Bea opened the door for them. "Yes, dear." She patted Georgie on the back. "I'm sure that place brings back memories, doesn't it? I remember you going down there every spare moment you had." Her voice was soft. Georgie stared, incapable of speaking, her throat tight, and her stomach hollow. She just stood there not sure what was supposed to come next, Ella nudging with her elbow, her hands full of enough sugar to put every kid in the village school on a high until Christmas.

"Sarah Dixon saw him dropping you off last night. Now you take care, won't you? And pop in again soon. And you watch yourself with that Jake Harcourt, although he's not the hell raiser he used to be."

Georgie tried to push the shock of where he was aside. Concentrate on what was really important. Okay, maybe they weren't witches, maybe just curtain twitching nosy neighbours. Thank Christ she hadn't kissed him, or, she gulped. She'd asked him in. Heaven help her if he'd said yes. They'd have made the front page of the local newspaper and given the town enough ammunition for the reverberations to get all the way back to Alfie.

Except she was an adult. She was allowed to ask who she wanted in. And if she wanted a wild ride on his motorbike then she was perfectly entitled to do that too.

Bugger.

"Georgie, Georgie." The sharp elbow in her ribs brought her back down to earth with an ouch. "What was all that about then? And can you grab some of these sweets off me please, pretty please?"

"You do realise you'll explode if you eat this lot?" Georgie put a handful of the sweets in her pocket and stared at Ella, determined to focus on her, and not an image of Jake on his motorbike, on Marsh Lane.

"Have you seen these—?"

"I don't want to see. I put on pounds just looking. I'll walk back with you, then I need to get the car."

"I'm coming too."

"Nope." She shook her head slowly to make sure Ella got the message. This was a trip down memory lane she had to take on her own. Firstly, because it was Rowena's place which could stir up feelings she was sure she didn't want to acknowledge, second because she had a horrible feeling the only plan she had for the future was about to be cocked up in a terminal way, and thirdly...

well, thirdly she didn't quite know what to make of the bad biker boy any more.

"Spoilsport."

"You got it." Next time she laid eyed on Jake Harcourt she wanted to be on her own, because every time the thought of that bike entered her head, which was pretty often, she felt an indescribable urge to be bad. Very bad.

***

Georgie had ditched the high heels in favour of a pair of old wellingtons she'd found in the outhouse and she'd pulled on an old sweater, jeans and a beret to keep her warm. The thick long scarf was because she hadn't got a baggy enough jacket to go over the rest. So not front-of-house.

She sauntered slowly up the lane feeling liberated in the flat boots. When was the last time she'd walked anywhere? When was the last time she'd pulled on scruffy old clothes and just relaxed? She couldn't remember. Life wasn't like that anymore.

One kick of the crisp brown mottled leaves in the air and she was thrown, instantly, painfully, back to being a child again. A laughing, joking Georgie being chased by her father down this lane. Thrown up in the air until she squealed.

Swallowing the pang of sadness down, she blinked hard to clear the mist from her eyes. It was too long ago, she shouldn't let an autumn day and walking down this oh so familiar lane affect her like that. It was just a road. It could be anywhere. But when she glanced up, the white puff balls of cloud scudding across a clear blue sky made her ache inside. A lump that hadn't been there for a long time clutched at her chest, tightened her throat until it was hard to swallow.

One day it had been normal. The next it was screaming and tears. She'd never heard her parents swear before, or even argue, but now they'd used up a lifetime's quota over the explosive week that it lasted. Then nothing. One last door banging and the war was over. A ghostly quiet and a father who systematically, scarily, smashed every plate in the house.

She'd wanted to yell at him to stop. But she didn't. Instead she ran away. Hid at the bottom of the garden under the safe canopy of trees until he came to find her. The next day he packaged her up like some unwanted gift that needed returning to the store. Took her away from her home, from her school, from her friends. Installed her somewhere bright, shiny and new. With the man who overnight had changed from the laughing dad into the alien Alfie and, too soon after, she'd been introduced to his dotty wife-to-be Carol.

She'd never even said goodbye to anyone or anything. That day he'd walked down the steps and put their suitcases in the boot of the car, rattled the gate to check it was secure then driven away without a backwards glance. The house that was her home had been locked up, locked out. Forgotten.

Her mother had never meant to get pregnant again, if she hadn't she probably would have never said she was leaving with her toy boy. The man who made her feel wanted. The man she bought a plane ticket with and never looked back.

But shit happens, and sometimes it keeps happening.

Georgie opened the eyes she hadn't realised she'd shut and looked down at the leaves round her feet. She stooped, picked up one of the shiny brown conkers from the road and rolled it round, the still waxy surface tacky against her fingertips, then closed her hand tight around it and shoved both her fists in her pockets. Slowing down to think about things was bad, ploughing on into the unknown, every day a different challenge was good. Kicking her way out of the crap that had closed in around her. She gave a last kick at the leaves, but this time it was an angry jab, that sent a pain though her toe. Great, just what she needed, a broken toe. She hobbled a couple of steps, at least this was a proper pain. Kicked her boot off and wiggled the toes experimentally, they moved so they couldn't be broken, could they? She pulled her wellie back on with a sigh. Dawdling was just putting off the moment when she'd get there. Have to face him again and work out how to get what she wanted. It was time to kick ass, if her foot was up to it.

"Bit of a coincidence isn't it? Twice in one week after not seeing you for years."

"How could I stay away?" Keep her tone light was one thing, keeping her eyes off him was something altogether different. No-one should be allowed to look like that, Georgie decided. But at least the dread in her stomach when she'd turned into the place had been replaced with little fingers of anticipation that were reaching down a bit lower.

From the shadow on his chin he couldn't have shaved since she last saw him, and the curls on his forehead were damp with perspiration. So was the black T-shirt that was clinging to his torso, just like she wanted to. He was gazing at her through dark lashes and the quirk to the corner of his mouth could have been amusement or something her dirty mind had made up.

Bugger.

"Did you forget something?" He'd ignored her comment, obviously used to being lusted after. But she was more than happy to up her game if she needed to.

"Call me nosy. I wondered what you got up to these days, when you weren't handing out rides."

This time he half grinned. What she was after, she supposed, except those little fingers in her stomach were firming up into more and tugging at something deep down in her stomach. Promising.

"I don't tend to hand out seconds."

"Arrogant bugger." She laughed and the other side of his mouth joined in with the grin.

"If you've got it, why deny it?" He held out his hands wide, as though in submission and chuckled. Lord that chuckle was dangerous, it was practically making her toes curl, and causing all kinds of other havoc on its way down there.

"So, what do you do?" She glanced around, so that she had an excuse not to carry on staring at him. Being lured in, she needed to control this. Not just jump the man. There were neat fields either side, a barn at the end of the track and not much else from what she could see. The same old place that she remembered from all those years ago, but tidier. The same post and rail fence, still with the teeth marks.

Exactly the same teeth marks. She stared. This was worse than she'd thought. Her fingers curled, tight in her pockets until her nails bit into the palms of her hands. He shouldn't be here, in this field. He should be in the next one along, nearer to Rowena's, further from her memories. This wasn't his place, it was hers. She bit the inside of her cheek and forced herself to stop looking at the stupid fence.

Looked at something new. A neat white line of electric tape around the gateway to stop it becoming a muddy morass. Not that mud had bothered her last time she was here.

"I fix horses."

"Fix? Come on, you're not a vet." He didn't even like horses, he'd never liked horses or she'd have noticed when they were kids. They'd been her whole life back then.

"Wow, as sharp as ever I see, Sherlock." He stuffed his hands in his pockets and stood square. Damn, she was back to staring at him. "I fix their heads not their bodies, it's all in the mind as they say."

"What is?"

"The bogeyman, the monster hiding in dark places. That irresistible urge to run hard and fast."

There was a trace of something darker in his voice, maybe something bitter, maybe just plain old irony. It wasn't there long enough to pin down, but she sensed it. He shrugged, dispersed the tension she was sure she hadn't imagined.

"Sometimes it can be a good idea to run." She tried to make a joke out of it, but his face didn't lift.

"Messes with your head if you don't know why you're running." His eyes narrowed, sending out a fan of fine wrinkles towards his temples.

And she knew if she came out with it straight, why she was there, he'd be the one running hard and fast. She hadn't quite worked out how to get round him yet, but the longer she looked at him the more she wanted him in the shoot. And she wanted it here too. It was part of him, and she didn't want to separate the two. And it was part of her, a part that the ache inside her might want back. A sticking plaster for the soul as her gran would have said.

"So, where are the horses?"

"She's in the barn."

"She? As in one horse? That's a bit crap isn't it, as businesses go?"

"It's how I work." He paused. "One at a time." Stared.

Now, was that a threat or a promise? He enunciated each syllable, slow and clear in that quiet, low tone of his and she suddenly knew that now might be the time to cut and run. To get away while she still wanted to. If she still wanted to.

Forget the whole thing. It was better to go somewhere else, get away from this stupid place. It was easy to find a man, a guy who looked good in dirty jeans, a grin and not much more. Very easy. A man with a dimple in the middle of his chin, and green brown eyes that you wanted to sink slowly into. A man with a firm body that you could wrap yourself round. Easy.

"I've got a proposition for you."

Chapter Three

He wasn't going to like this. She didn't like it. What in the world had made her say it? Well she knew the answer to that one. He turned her on. He intrigued her. Having men like Jake in her life was what kept her going. He was unpredictable and just looking at him gave her a thrill, oh yeah, and just imagining what he might do to her next, that was what made her determined not to let him disappear from her life yet.

"Shall I just say no now, and shortcut the process?"

"No, let's not. Don't say anything. Just listen until I've told you what it is."

He leaned back against the fence, stretched one leg out, so that his thigh muscles lengthened, long and taut against the worn denim of his jeans. She could run her hand down that thigh and it would be rock hard. Like something else by the looks of him.

"I've got another job."

"Busy girl."

She ignored that. "I scout for this agency that does photo shoots."

"No." He straightened, folded his arms across his chest and everything about him said no. "You're not bringing them here."

Why bother denying it? "Why not? They'll pay. It's good money."

"You'll disturb the horses."

"Horse."

He shrugged.

"We pay quite a lot." Safer to work on the location bit, then bring in the trickier 'him being in shot' bit later.

She'd called in to see Rowena on the way up, checked that Jake would be where she thought he was, and it had been nice to see the older woman. She'd been made to feel welcome, wanted, a feeling she hadn't had for a long time. Rowena had laughed though when she'd told her why she was there. "I've no objections to your friends taking a few photographs up there, love. But I can't speak for Jake and as he's paying the rent, he does have the last say, despite the past." She'd put a finger under Georgie's chin and studied her for a moment. "He's no pushover though, not even for a pretty face. You go ahead and ask, it might do him good." It had been on the tip of Georgie's tongue to ask what she meant, but she'd bit it back. She didn't want to get into discussions about the past. And she hadn't liked the 'good luck' and chuckle thrown after her as she'd pulled the gate shut.

Jake gave a short humourless laugh. "However much it is, it's not enough." He held up a hand to stop her objection. "Not everyone has a price, Georgie. I thought you'd have learned that by now. You can't just buy your way in, I'm not for sale."

"Ahh, come on, name your price, it doesn't have to be money, anything." There had to be a way, he had to agree, let her do the shoot here. "Just a couple of hours, a few piccies."

"You can't afford me, Georgie girl."

"Try me." He would let her. She could almost taste victory. He'd moved on from the straight no.

He met her stare, his eyes dark, hooded. "I thought I'd done that."

"Funny. Stop giving me your horny look and stop trying to change the subject."

He laughed out loud then. "I wonder just how far you'd go, to get your own way?"

"You won't know unless you ask."

He was looking amused now, almost like he'd realised he could have fun. It should have made her apprehensive, but come on what could he possibly come up with that could be that hard to sort? At least he'd given up on the grumpiness and gone back to the happy go lucky Jake she loved. She thought.

He was smiling, broad, real with a hint of tease. "I remember you when you used to spend all weekend playing with ponies."

Huh-huh. Slight change of tack in the wind.

"And?"

"I could do with a hand, well more like a nice pair of legs and a sticky bum." He grinned, all wolfish and bad. His gaze drifted over her body, slowly oh so slowly down her legs and she fought the impulse to fidget. He was getting into this. "Okay, here's the deal. Let's see you do some grafting for a change."

She shrugged. Refused to rise to the bait. She grafted, he'd no idea the hours she'd put in, maybe not with physical work like he did. So what? Hard work didn't have to involve breaking your back and ruining your fingernails.

"You give me a hand with the horses, just for the next few weeks. Say six? I know you can handle them, I remember that black mare you used to have and the amount of bouncing about you did on her." He was still grinning, his head tipped to one side. "And off her." There was a challenge in those gorgeous green eyes.

Boy, yeah, she remembered that mare. She'd never been thrown off an animal so many times in her life, bouncing just wasn't the word for it, but she'd kept going back for more. And in the end they'd reached a truce. "Horse. You've only got one to help with." This could be a win, win. She got her shoot, a sexy guy on tap for a while, and a chance to exorcise the last unwanted part of this place from her brain. But let him think he was driving a hard bargain.

"I've got a long list of people waiting and I do home visits as well. I can get through them quicker if I've got a," he paused, raised an eyebrow as though challenging her, "groom to help."

"Don't push it, I'm nobody's slave labour." But she needed to know there'd be something to do or she'd be bored rigid. And wound up about being here. I mean they couldn't just shag all day, could they?

He grinned. "No, can't picture you as a willing slave, maybe an unwilling one."

"Stop it, you're doing it again."

"I could just do with another pair of hands, some of these horses are tricky and the owners are worse than useless. That's if you don't mind a hard ride?"

"Hard suits me fine." She smiled back, she couldn't help it. "Oh well, at least I rank above worse than useless, maybe at just useless?"

"Your choice."

Don't rush it. Play hard to get for once. Count to ten, well five. "Four weeks. And I'd need to work it round my other jobs."

"I know. But it's six weeks, I've got jobs lined up that need clearing before the weather gets tricky. Take it or leave it. I'm sure I can find someone else if you're not interested."

"Five weeks," wait for it, don't lose it now, "but I need you to do something else as well." She wasn't going to smile, not yet.

"Five weeks without the something else, six weeks with."

Shit, since when had bad boy Jake turned into Mr Unyielding businessman? "Done." She held out a hand before he could change the rules, ask about the something else.

"And I get to do the horny look whenever I want." He moved off the fence, wrapped his warm, firm fingers around hers and she stared straight into those mossy eyes. Oh yeah, she could cope with the horny look. "And to think about you being my unwilling slave."

"Do all the thinking you like buster. I do the six weeks, we do the shoot here and," she resisted the urge to cling onto his hand, "you are in the frame." She tried not to giggle or whoop.

***

"And what the hell does that mean?" Jake knew he was frowning, and had a horrible feeling he was glaring. He'd come up with the stupid deal on the spur of the moment, not really thinking, just sure that working with the horses would be beneath her. At school she'd been different. Quiet, unassuming, despite the fact that her family obviously had more money to throw around than he'd ever see in a lifetime. But she'd changed, hardened and he didn't know how deep it went. He'd admired the way she'd handled her horse, but not been under any illusions, for all he knew she'd had an army of grooms at her disposal. But, he wanted her to know that getting what you want sometimes had strings attached. He wasn't the pushover she was used to, however much she batted her eyelids and thrust those slim hips his way. She was desperate to use this place, he'd seen it in the clenched fists, the casual tone that wasn't. Which struck him as odd and he had to admit he was curious, even though he had a rule never to be curious about anything.

He'd met girls like the grown up Georgina before though, the too posh to push brigade. Girls like her looked down on people like him, used them for their own cheap thrills then bleated about being used as an excuse to run away and not face up to the truth.

Well, he wasn't after her money, and he didn't want her and a crowd of glamour pusses treating the countryside like a giant novelty ride. But, he had felt sorry for the look he'd left on her face when he'd driven off last night. She'd looked lost, vulnerable and he'd regretted suggesting she'd turned into one of the 'having it all' brats. And in the back of his mind, niggling away, was the image of her at school. Her head always buried in a book, the long hair masking her face. She'd been an innocent back then, and more times than not he'd caught her looking at him and he'd purposefully blanked her. She was out of his league.

He remembered speaking to her once, once in all the time he'd been aware of her. Normally she'd been pretty self-contained, but this time the look in her eye had been almost desperate. Like she wanted to reach out, but she daren't. And he'd recognised himself for a moment. And so he'd told her what he'd told himself, to stop waiting and watching. To just get on with it. He'd only seen her a handful of times after that, and he'd avoided talking. What was the point? And then she'd gone. Just like that. Overnight. Story of his life.

He'd had it all once, well enough if not all. Then watched his useless father throw it all away. Burn every memory he'd ever had. He'd as good as lost both his parents in a single day, and he'd sworn as a teenager that he'd never let it happen again. There wouldn't be anything to lose in his life, no-one to let down. Ignoring the sweet Georgina had been the only thing to do back then. Playing around with the girls who just wanted a good time worked fine, just fine. No expectations. Nothing to live up to. And now, it seemed the grown up Georgie would be tough enough to understand.

And he'd somehow agreed to let her use him. She'd turned the tables, or at least they were at a status quo. And a status quo with the polished brunette she'd turned into couldn't be all bad.

"It means" he could have sworn those brown eyes were flashing with some inner light of laughter, "that you're in some of the shots."

"And you used to be such a nice girl, play fair."

"And now I'm all grown up." She grinned. "And I play to win, Mr Horny."

He laughed, he couldn't help himself. "I'm not getting all tarted up just to give you a laugh."

"Don't worry." She put both her hands on his chest, long fingers splayed out, all the tension had leached out of her the second he'd said yes. "I like you just the way you are."

"Seriously, I don't do photo's."

"Seriously, you need to trust me on this one." He resisted the urge to cover her hands with his. Apart from having a crazy, irrational desire to give her the good spanking she deserved, he really shouldn't go there. "Tuesday work for you?"

"I'll check if I have a window in my diary." He kept his hands off her, fisted at his sides, his tone dry.

"Oh yeah?" She was grinning again, and this close it was having a funny effect on his groin, all the blood that should have been helping his head out was heading straight down south. He could lean in just a bit, kiss that cute upturned nose. "You do that mister." She dropped her hands, took a step back and the spell was broken, except for that dark look in her eyes that was longing or just plain lust.

He stared and she stared straight back. And his cock jumped a little bit more to attention.

"I better go." She didn't move.

"You had." He could hear the need in her voice, hear the break in his own. One step was all he had to take, but he wasn't going to.

She hesitated, long enough to give him a chance and he stood frozen, willing her to walk. Then she did, turned on her heel and set off down the long driveway, swinging her hips in time with the long strides.

Georgina was all grown up, and she'd grown up as trouble. The type of trouble that had always tempted a man like him. And he would have grabbed it with both hands, except he remembered the girl she used to be. And he remembered the life he used to have. And he wasn't going back.

***

There was that end of October chill in the air when Georgie cycled up the long driveway to the barn. She dumped the bike against the fence and rubbed her hands together, breathing hard so she could watch the warm air clash with the cold. It gave her a weird kind of satisfaction to just stand there and blow out hot air.

"Early bird."

She stopped the childish game abruptly and shoved her hands into the pockets of her corduroys.

"Doing your bit towards saving the planet?" He nodded towards the bike, smiled so that the dimple in his chin deepened. "Miss

Eco-friendly on your green machine, eh?"

"Well I thought I had to do something to combat your motorbike fumes."

He'd got a t-shirt on, stretched tight over his broad chest, showcasing his pecs, the short sleeves showing off the strong biceps, triceps and every other muscle she could think of. Well, she'd just about reached her limit with muscle identification, but she was sure that every one that should be there was, in all its well defined glory.

The heat brushed along her cheekbones as she realised she was studying him, and he was waiting. Looking amused.

"Aren't you cold?" It came out a bit sharp, defensive, and his grin widened.

"I've been mucking out, worked up quite a sweat actually." He raised an eyebrow. "Might have to strip down further."

"Stop that." She was tempted to ask what had got into him this morning, but not very tempted. Asking would probably throw the off switch and put him back into defensive mode, and this type of attack was far nicer.

"In fact," he took another step, which brought him perilously close, reached out to grab hold of her scarf, "I might have to strip you down a bit as well."

Except they'd have company soon and she could look so unprofessional. "You're rude." She put her own hand on the scarf, just in case he carried out the threat.

"Very. And I thought you were too."

"They'll be here any minute."

"It need only take a minute, makes it more exciting." He tugged the one end of the scarf with a little pull she felt right through her body. Raised his eyebrows. "Not knowing who might be watching."

She was tempted, very tempted. Her pussy was already tightening with anticipation. He leaned in, nudged the scarf away from her neck. His breath heating her skin just before the warm dampness of his mouth bathed it.

"You are bad." It came out on a gasp of a moan as he sucked gently right at the most sensitive spot, she tipped her head willing him on. They might not get caught.

"I am." He sucked harder. "I don't do boring."

Oh, God she could feel her knickers getting damper by the minute. What if they did get caught? His hand cupped her breast and even through the thickness of t-shirt and jumper she could feel the heat, feel the brush of his thumb against her nipple as though she were naked.

He pulled back a bit, chuckled, looked her straight in the eye. "Oh, Georgie girl, who'd have thought?" Then his firm lips came down hard over her mouth and she forgot all about wondering who'd have thought what. His tongue played with hers, danced along the edge of her teeth and just as she started to join in he pulled back from the bruising kiss, left her mouth and other parts of her body tingling.

His finger rested under her chin, his gaze was fixed on her lips, and she was pretty sure she was swaying towards him, but he just smiled. A slow, lazy smile, and his voice when it came was a gentle drawl that wrapped around her senses.

"I think the cavalry have arrived to save you."

She jumped, literally jumped away from him and his mouth twitched at the corners.

"I'll get my own back over this you know." He shook his head slowly. "In the frame my arse."

"Well I wasn't thinking of having that particular part of your anatomy in the shot, but if you're offering?"

He wasn't it seemed. But he did do what he was asked, lounged against the fence and looked sexy in the background. He even spun a rope, but he refused point blank when they asked him to get on his horse.

"The horse isn't part of the bargain."

Georgie frowned. "Negotiate?"

"No negotiations." He shook his head. She could have suggested the motorbike, but she kept her mouth zipped on that one. It would have been too much to see him posing on the big black beast, stroking a hand along the tank, and he knew it. He winked when her gaze flicked towards it and back. Grinned when her mouth clamped shut.

"You could just hold the mare?"

"Nope. She's been fucked up enough without seeing you lot."

Toby had laughed, but she hadn't. It was a good idea and he was just being awkward, proving she couldn't push him around.

She tried to take a step back. She didn't need to be involved, she didn't have to let him get to her, this was Toby's gig, let him do the arguing. Her end of the deal had been to set up the shoot, and she'd delivered. End of.

She could relax, try and let the beauty of the autumn morning seep into her soul like it used to do. The heavy dew was still clinging to the blades of grass as lunchtime approached, dark trails skating across the field, showing where they'd been. She'd always liked autumn, it was mellow, thoughtful. The colours of red and gold, brown and green soft in the gentle rays of sunlight. Her favourite time of the year to paint, when you lost the harshness, the definition of life, of everything.

Autumn was gentle, and autumn could be sad. When she glanced up he was watching her. He was so still, as though paused in time, but his eyes never stopped and nor she suspected did his mind. Jake was sharp, dangerous.

She purposefully kept away from him as they broke off for a quick break to regroup. She collared Toby, suggested a new spot to take some photographs. But she couldn't block Jake out completely, whatever she was doing, however engrossed she was. He was there. A presence.

She shook her head to clear it, bent down to pick up one of the camera bags. Work first, deal with him later. This place had brought back too many memories, put her on edge, spooked her out. That was all it was. She was just more aware of everything.

Not just him.

"You have so come up trumps, girl." Ella was grinning. "Awesome."

They stood together, watched as Jake leant casually against the fence, one foot up on a rail as instructed and sent her a wink that put her body back on full alert. Then he ruffled up his hair as instructed by the makeup girl and Georgie could almost feel the cringe as his nose was dabbed with foundation powder.

"I know. I'm always awesome." Georgie fought the grin that was threatening to split her face open. Not cool. She tore her gaze from Jake, that look of resigned humour that had settled on his features was the look she wanted to see when she seduced him later. And she was going to have him again, she'd decided.

"And wouldn't you like to rip his clothes off and lick him all over?"

"Ella!"

Ella carried on gazing at Jake like she believed in love at first sight. "Oops, sorry, forgot you already had. Do you think we could get Toby to ask him to take his shirt off? Or at least unbutton it a bit. If you don't mind that is?"

"Go ahead, he's not my personal property." But even as she said it she knew she was kidding herself. She didn't want him stripped, centre stage, for the models to fawn over. A brooding presence in the background was just fine. "Jake might object though, even if Toby doesn't."

"I think I might ask him while he's setting the next shot up. Come on." She linked her arm through Georgie's, so she didn't have much choice.

Toby carried on adjusting the lights and reflectors as they got close, flashed a quick smile in her direction. "This place is fab, George. A real prime location."

"Thanks, Toby. It's great isn't it?"

"Cool. And that guy is something else as well, he's a natural. You've done a good job this time."

"Thanks."

"Yeah, the girls just love your macho man." The words were laced with dry humour. That was Toby all over, dry as dust. It had taken her a while to get used to him, to work out if he was serious or joking, and she still wasn't always sure she'd got it right.

He nodded over in the direction of his models, who had taken time off to grab a drink. And more. Yeah, they sure did love him. Especially Cara, if she pressed herself in any closer she'd need pulling off like a sticking plaster. "He's not mine." Something tugged at her deep inside, it must be impatience. She just wanted them to get on with it, finish their break and get back to work. Cara in the front of the shot, Jake at the back. With his shirt still on.

"Let's hope the prints look as good as I'm hoping they will."

She quelled the sudden irritation that had broken into the happy feeling of getting it right, achieving something.

"You could make something of this land," Toby tightened a furled knob on the light and stepped back to check it, "I'd definitely use it again. But do you think macho man would let me? He doesn't seem over keen, he really gave me the evil eye before. He is great for the photos though, talk about brooding, he has got it in spades. People are falling over themselves for that rough, tough look at the moment."

"No, he's not keen." It didn't take Einstein to work that one out. "But it isn't his to decide. I bet I can sort something, so maybe we could do a deal." Now where the hell had that come from? Sort something? It had been hers once, theirs. The best part of her childhood. But that had been then, this was now. It had been a shock coming back, the way it hit her. The house wasn't her home now, it had been defiled. Spoiled forever. But this place hadn't.

"Wow, you really are the country bumpkin at heart aren't you?"

She blinked. What the hell was she thinking, saying it out loud? It wasn't her place now, and something kept niggling at her saying she couldn't go back. Going back never worked. But when she'd told Alfie she was heading home for the summer it was for one reason. This place. A memory she couldn't shake, an idea that had grown inside her until it had seemed real. Until she'd got back and found Jake here.

Toby high fived her. "Here's to a deal then darling."

She tried her best at a weak grin and then out of the corner of her eye saw him. Felt the smile suddenly fix itself on her face like a brittle mask. He was a few feet away, had walked back their way while she was distracted. While the thoughts that had been filtering through her brain ever since she'd step foot back on the land had coagulated into the start of a plan without her really knowing. And from the look on his face he'd heard every word. Every single word. And the look he gave her was more than just distaste, it was disgust mingled with pity. If she'd thought she'd been hurt in the past, it was nothing compared to what that one single look threatened. Fuck. That wasn't supposed to happen. It wasn't supposed to happen at all.

Chapter Four

"They're all assholes." She could see the pulse under his tense jaw, he was fighting for control.

The assholes were busy packing their stuff away. "Well get used to it, because they'll be back." Shit, why was she winding him up? Apart from the fact that he was so sexy when he was about to let rip. She could almost see the tightening of his abs, the flex of the muscles in his arms. The green in his eyes had gone from soft inviting moss to hard jade that could cut straight through the crap, to the very core of you.

"Oh, yeah? Well, it isn't your place to decide."

"And it's not yours. Is it, Jake?" She squared up to him, refused to step away like her brain was telling her to.

"So how are you planning to sort it, then Georgie? Shag me into submission? Could be fun trying."

She didn't like the smile that was playing on his lips. It was him goading her now.

"Dream on."

"At least I'm in on the game plan now, makes it fairer."

"Sod off. There isn't a game plan."

He raised an eyebrow.

"I'm not one of your play things, Georgie."

Hot tears prickled behind her eyes. He was wrong, he had it

all wrong. But how the hell could she even start to explain? She didn't even know herself why she'd said it, didn't even know what she really meant any more. She'd come back expecting to find this land empty, abandoned. Just how she'd left it. Jake wasn't supposed to be here. Nobody was supposed to be here. And no-one was supposed to know about her plan. Not yet.

"You can't walk all over Rowena like you do with everyone else. She's a match for you, lady." The short, humourless laugh filled the gap between them. Brittle. Challenging.

"She knows what this place means to me." She clamped her lips together too late to stop the words spilling out.

"Which is what exactly?" He crossed the broad arms across his chest and she studied the dark hairs that moved with each irate flex of his muscles. Saved her from looking at the granite features.

"That black mare? Well, I kept her here."

"So? You rented the place, now I am."

"No." She swallowed the need down, fought the desperation that she knew would creep into her voice if she wasn't careful. "No, we owned the place. Dad owned it." She glanced up and his face was stormy, unreadable. "Honest, we did. And I think we still do." Shut up Georgie, why can't you just keep your mouth shut, at least until you've got all the facts? But the words just spilled out, as though saying them would help make the dreams that had been brewing into a reality she suddenly needed.

"Well, bully for you little rich girl." His eyes had narrowed and it was like looking into a bottomless pit, nothing. Emptiness. "Even," he paused, "even if you're right, Rowena has an agreement, I have an agreement." He reached into his pocket, dug out a mobile phone.

"What are you doing?"

"Proving you can't have everything you want at a drop of a hat." He pressed a handful of buttons, held the phone to his ear. "Rowena?"

Georgie fought the urge to shut her eyes. Just like that the harsh tone had melted into the smooth warmth he'd had for her when she'd got there this morning.

"It's Jake, I've got Georgina Hampton here, she seems to think," his steely gaze never left her, "I have no right to be here."

"I never said—" He ignored her.

"Can we have a chat when you've got a minute?" The slightest curl tilted the corner of his mouth as he ended the call, which was obviously just leaving a message. The phone was pocketed, and his hand went with it as he rocked slightly back on his heels with what looked like a hint of smug satisfaction. "We all can."

"We all can what? There is no 'we'. You can't decide for me what I'm going to do."

"Watch me." He raised an eyebrow and she felt her mouth open and snap shut of its own accord. Bloody stupid macho man, no-one told her what to do. No-one.

"You don't even like horses."

"Oh, yeah?"

"You don't, you never rode, I never saw you." Okay, she sounded childish. Even to her own ears.

"Not at your posh little girl gymkhanas maybe. But some things are in the blood."

"Oh, just—" Just what? She glared at him and he looked straight back like he knew he had an advantage. "Just fuck off. I'm going. This is ridiculous, you're ridiculous." She half spun round but he'd got a hold of her arm before she made it all the way. "Let go of me."

"You started this, Georgina." He voice was low, a warning. But she didn't care, for a start he was just trying to needle her calling her Georgina.

"Oh, and you think you can finish *it* do you, Jake Harcourt? Whatever *it* is?"

"Stop acting like a spoiled brat." His voice was as hard as his eyes.

"Stop behaving like a caveman, and let go of my frigging arm."

"Whatever you're plotting in that mad head of yours we're going to sort it. After you've done a mornings work for me."

"Fuck off." She could almost hear her own teeth grinding

together as she spat the words out. Work for the overbearing lunatic? Who did he think he was?

"Tut, tut. The old Georgina would have stuck to her side of the bargain."

"Well, I'm not the old bloody Georgina, am I?" She tried to shake her arm free, but he didn't let go.

"No, I guess you're not." He slowly released his grip. In his own time. Let his arm drop down to his side, the soft tone no longer a warning. "More fool me."

She took a step away, out of his range. "I'll be here at six, happy now?" She would stick to her side of the bargain. Whatever he thought of her, she always did what she said she would. Even if it would be like pulling teeth, slowly, without the aid of an anaesthetic. And if he tried to push it and say earlier than six he was a dead man. "And it's Georgie, okay? Call me Georgie."

"Don't forget your bike."

Shit, she had been so intent on marching away on a self-righteous note that she'd very nearly set off down the lane without it.

By the time she'd grabbed the bike and wheeled it up from the barn, he'd gone. Which was good, because she didn't want to see the pompous over-bearing twit ever again, and tomorrow morning would come round far too quickly.

***

Why the hell had she said to Toby that she'd sort something? Jake had been wrong, so wrong when he assumed she had a plan to seduce him, persuade him to let them come back. That idea hadn't even been on the distant horizon. Until he'd said it the thought had never entered into her head. No, a far more dangerous one had. That distant, niggling need to get this place back had sneaked up on her a while ago and she hadn't been able to shake it off. Coming back had been the first step, a chance to look around, plan the future that the past had forced her to abandon.

And all of a sudden she'd been convinced she could do it. She was mad. It had just come out of the blue, one moment she'd been wishing herself back to the time she'd spent the days up here with her Dad. Thinking that if she could just come back here she could somehow fix things. Come back to the point where it had all started to go wrong, but this time take a different path. Then, the next minute, the stupid thoughts had shot out of her dumb mouth in a string of useless words.

He wasn't supposed to be here. No-one was supposed to be here.

And he'd heard. Why the fuck had he been stood there listening? If he hadn't, she could have thought about it. Talked herself out of the mad plan that was bubbling around and forming itself into a map of the future. But how could she do that now? And he'd rung bloody Rowena, roped her in and made it look like she was a selfish cow just sweeping her way in and knocking him out of the way. And she wasn't. Was she? This place was hers, a part of her, and if she could only stay she could sort herself out. Start over.

She stopped pedalling, slowed to a halt and slipped off the seat of the bike, her hands tightening on the handle bars. She wasn't being selfish. She wasn't. Something deep down inside her wanted this place, needed it. Even if it all seemed so much more complicated now than that hazy dream in her head,

And Rowena had lots of land. Her house was next to the smallholding and surrounded by fields. She must have agreed to take this one on when Alfie had done his moonlight flit. Her dad, Alfie, wouldn't have sold it. Rowena had probably offered to rent it, look after it to stop gypsies moving in, or property developers trying to buy it. That would be all. And she could give Jake another field, another barn. This one didn't mean anything to him, it was just a field.

She rested her chin on her hands and stared blankly at the road ahead. It had hit her like a thump in the gut when she'd stopped by at Rowena's asking about Jake. When she'd realised just exactly where he was. In the one untouched part of her childhood memories. And as she'd made her way up, each step had got harder, the dread slowly building. And when she'd got to the gate it was there, exactly as she remembered. Down to every last gouge that her mare had made in the fence. Maybe it would have been better if it hadn't been. If the dream had already been destroyed.

Prime location Toby had said. The words etched themselves into her brain. But it wasn't just that. It was a part of her, a part of her past that had been dropped abruptly back into her present, and she felt like turning her back on it would rip the last part of her old life from her heart. Coming back she'd felt, just for a fleeting moment, like the girl she used to be; a girl with a loving father, and a mother who was always there for her. And it had felt more real than anything had in a long time.

Georgie had never really stopped still long enough to question whether she believed in fate, and she didn't think everything happened for a reason. What the hell kind of reason was there for her mum getting screwed by a man who wasn't much older than her daughter? But being here seemed to have put a roadblock in front of her. Stopped the run of her life. Signposted a diversion. And she wanted to stay put.

No, she didn't. She fought the sudden urge to whimper and wail. It wasn't that. She didn't want to curl up here and hide from reality, pretend it hadn't happened. It could be her way of making a decent living; that was what it was all about. If she had this land back, she had the start of something. She could do something, anything. Rent it to Toby. Get a horse, give lessons again. Anything. And she could hold up the fingers to catty Carol and prove to her father she could make it on her own. No more relying on them, no more putting up with the snide comments. And when Carol insisted on selling the house, which she knew was coming any day now, she'd have somewhere she could use as her art studio. Yes, that was it. She could set up a studio in the barn as well, and do what she wanted with her life, not what they wanted. They could sod 'going back to discuss things', which was Carol speak for, come and work for your father and do as you're told young lady.

She'd known when she'd got the job at The Veneto that it wouldn't be enough, and nor would the work with Toby. They wanted more, a career, a bloody life plan. I mean, who wanted a 'life plan'?

She scuffed her boot against the grass verge. A base here would be good, if Toby made some bookings, and spread the word, and she had a studio set up in the barn, and she could even let Jake rent the land off her for a bit as well. She could have other horses, or give lessons or something. Yeah, if she could put up with the sanctimonious looks from Jake, God that man had an almighty boulder on his shoulder. Who was he to judge her? What exactly had he done in his life that gave him the moral high ground?

Georgie spun the pedal slowly back on the bike. Maybe it wasn't such a mad idea after all. One call was all she had to make, one call to Alfie and she could find out if they still owned the place or whether he'd sold out to Rowena. Sold off another chunk of her life.

Sod him, she wasn't going to ask. Not yet. Instead she dialled up Ella. The one person who wouldn't judge her on the past.

"What would you say if I told you I was going to buy this patch of land we did the shoot on?"

"What do you mean, buy it? You're mad. What do you want with a stupid field, girl?" Well, she'd been relying on Ella to be up front and direct, but maybe not this direct.

"It's not stupid, and I can do something with it. Build up a business."

"Like what exactly?"

"Well Toby said he'd be interested, he thinks it's a good idea. And I do need a place."

"He always says that, just in case it turns out to be."

"Thanks for the support."

"But you can't even live there, there isn't a house."

"There's a caravan."

"A caravan." Ella had gone very high pitched, all the way up to screech level. Followed be a raucous laugh. "You, in a caravan?"

Okay that sounded crazy even to her. "And there's a groom's flat in the barn. I just want it, Ella." She was beginning to sound like a six year old kid begging for a puppy.

"Does biker boy get thrown in as part of the bargain?"

"Very funny."

"You like him."

"So?"

"It's a field. Georgie. An overgrown lawn."

"It was my field."

Ella's sigh travelled across cyberspace. She wasn't laughing any more. "We're going out for a drink tonight and getting to the bottom of this."

***

Jake didn't want to watch her leave, because he'd be tempted to stop her. So he headed over to the small tack room at the back of the barn. What was it about the girl that meant he either had his hackles up, or an urge to pin her against the fence and shag her senseless? Well, he could figure the second part. But what was there to care about enough to annoy him? True, he liked a challenge but this was getting ridiculous. She just kept creeping under his skin and winding him up. One minute he had to admit to himself he liked her, the next he wanted to give her a good shaking. He couldn't even decide if she was smart or was completely off her rocker.

When she'd arrived there had been a hint of the old Georgie, uncomplicated, fun, wrapped up in a ridiculous scarf and old clothes that made her a thousand times more gorgeous than her normal get up. Then it had started. The crew had got on his wick, all pretensions and thinking they could order him about in his own place. And she'd been flirting away with the slime-ball in a way that made his teeth grind. But she'd topped it all, boy had she topped it all, when she'd come out with the statement about 'sorting it'.

He'd jumped to the conclusion that she was just confident she could seduce him into doing whatever she wanted. That had been bad, but the truth when it came out had been worse. She wanted to take the place, his place, on. Buy it from underneath him. Like she owned the whole frigging village. Which her dad probably damned near did. What was it with people who had it all, that they just wanted more? They didn't stop until they'd bled you dry, then moved on to the next poor idiot.

Yeah, whatever else he had to admit she was fit. But, so what? They were miles apart, she was a stuck up spoiled girl who thought she could do what she wanted, have it all, and he was the bit of rough she thought she could play with. He realised his face was set in a grimace. Which made his stomach muscles tighten that bit more. It didn't matter what she was after, she was nothing to him. They'd both ended up in the same spot when they needed a quick fix, and they'd got it. Then he'd dropped her off home and drove away, like he always did. End of.

He pulled on the black leather jacket, zipped it up abruptly. He needed a beer and a girl who didn't ask questions, who just wanted fun. A girl who wasn't out to wind him up or prove herself.

The motorbike roared into life the moment he touched it, he shoved it back off the stand and snapped his visor down. And tried not to remember what the touch of her hands had felt like, what the whisper of her breath down his neck had done to him as they'd powered down the lanes. His body have never been more aware of a woman's before, he'd never felt so desperate to see through what they'd started quite like he had that night. And that sweet glance of uncertainty she'd given him, mingled with a need he reckoned matched his own, had nearly tipped him over the edge before he'd started.

She'd long since gone when he reached the lane. It was empty, no sign of a girl in oversize muddy wellies and a scarf that was big enough for two. He revved the engine, debated what to do, and then turned up the lane towards the start of the urban sprawl. He'd get some air first, blow the anger away. There was something about his bike that soothed him, the power that threatened to burst free, pushing himself to the edge as the tarmac fled below the wheels.

The machine was warm beneath him when he finally slowed and pulled up, the slight tremor in his muscles replacing the tension of before. He took a deep breath, a mix of rubber, hot oil and fresh air filling his lungs, then pulled his helmet off and ran his fingers through his hair. The early evening air had the same cold tinge that had been there first thing, fingers of ice that stroked along his cheekbones. A sharp chill that snaked inside him with each deep breath, that made him feel alive.

The houses sprawled out below, a sprinkling of lights high spots in the gloom. He always felt strangely detached when he came up here. He didn't belong in this place any more, a place he hadn't managed to walk away from. He hadn't belonged since that day long ago when the man he had once been proud to call Dad had lit a match and dropped it into a pool of petrol.

In one night it had all gone, filtered into the universe. His favourite CD's, music player, best shirt, the football programme from when he'd been to Wembley. Every bit of crap that shouldn't have mattered. Including his roots. His parents. And now he didn't own anything. Or anyone.

But, with Rowena he'd found a kind of home. A non-demanding bolt hole that he could walk away from at any time. Except today he'd discovered he wasn't ready to walk. And it wasn't just because Georgina bloody Hampton had riled him. He owed it to Rowena to stick things out, they supported each other. She knew she had someone to call on if there was a problem. She might come over all tough, but he knew she was feeling her age, feeling exposed miles from the nearest neighbours. Yes, she had friends, lot of friends, but she was too proud to admit when things were getting tough.

And he noticed when a fence got broken, saw when her gutters were blocked. He owed her for the past and he wasn't about to walk away now and abandon her.

And he liked the place, and the horses.

He felt the smile tease at his mouth and suddenly realised he'd completely relaxed. It could be fun having a head to head with Georgie. There were brief moments when he saw the insecurity she used to have at school, the guarded expression, the complete lack of awareness of how she affected him. But now there was something else thrown into the mix, the confidence borne of money, the challenge she seemed to be throwing out at the world. Georgie didn't know who she was, didn't know what she wanted, but the aura of inhibition that had once cloaked her had gone. The grown up Georgie had a wild side, and he quite liked the idea of exploring it a bit.

A chuckle tickled deep down in his chest. She'd been throwing out a challenge to him at every opportunity, and she'd also been throwing out an invite. And he liked the idea of both. Georgie wanted a fight and she wanted fun, and he was going to be more than happy to supply both. She wouldn't know what had hit her protected little world.

There was more of a chill in the air than was welcome now and he didn't need to look at his watch to know he'd been sat for longer than he should. He started the bike up, but when he revved it this time, it was just to feel the pull, the roar of contained power. He fastened the jacket at the collar, shutting out the cold air and set off back down to the town towards a pint of beer that had his name on.

***

"Thought you were giving us a miss?"

"Heard there was a girl on the scene."

He ignored the comments and signalled the barman for a pint,

53

then raised the glass to his two oldest mates. "A right comedy double act you two are getting to be."

"Well?" Steve was cradling his own glass and waiting. "The girl?"

Jake raised an eyebrow. "Now who told you that?"

"There's a rumour going round town that you had her on your bike you dirty dog." Andy had joined in. "Wanted a bit of your throbbing machine did she?" Both men laughed.

The three of them went back years, long enough to say what they liked, half in jest, half serious. They drank together, went to football matches together, even occasionally did dating together. Though Andy always said that taking Jake anywhere was a mistake, because he was never serious about the woman he had with him, and the other women were always eyeing him up like they wouldn't say no. It shouldn't have been good for their egos, except they all knew the rules, all played fair.

"She wanted," Jake let the cool beer slip down his throat. Smooth, mellow, just what he needed, "a trip down memory lane, I think."

"She's an ex? I've never seen you with her before, you kept that one quiet."

"Remember mousy Georgina Hampton at school?"

Steve shook his head. "Nope."

"The swotty one who did your homework?"

Andy laughed again. "They all did his homework at some time or another."

It was obviously just him that remembered. The quiet girl who had studied them, that dark gaze darting away whenever he caught her in the act.

"You mean that one whose dad was a governor?"

"That's the one." Jake drained the rest of his pint.

"Don't remember her looking like that."

"Nope."

"Not turned out as frigid as she used to be then?"

"Nope." He took the fresh pint that Andy held out. Strange

thing was, she never had looked frigid to him. Shy, vulnerable, beautiful in an almost other-worldly way. Once or twice he'd hesitated, almost spoken to her, almost asked her what she was thinking about. But girls like her didn't need guys like him. And guys like him didn't ask questions like that.

"Fancy introducing us when you get fed up with her? Hey, did you see that goal?" They all looked up at the widescreen TV at the side of the bar. "What a corker." All eyes trained on the replay and talk turned to football and work, and when Jake was going to stop pissing about with horses and get a proper job. And how Andy was going to cope with fatherhood.

He'd been the first of them to go steady, the first to propose, and the first to get a mortgage. Jake was happy for him. It wasn't his bag, but he knew that his mate was content. For some people a home to go to, a family, steady income, nice car meant that life was good. But not for him. If you didn't wake up to the same thing every day, then you had nothing to miss when it went, did you?

"So, you seeing the school swot again?"

"Well, yes actually. She's going to work for me."

"You're kidding." Both men stopped drinking and stared. "Why the hell would she want to do that? Is she desperate?" Steve's baritone chuckle stopped the bar noise dead.

"Maybe she's after some more bike action." He made a revving up gesture.

Andy frowned. "She looked hot. You sure it was the same girl?"

Jake felt the tremble of his phone vibrating in his pocket, fished it out. A text. *'A gentleman never talks about his shags.'* Some instinct told him which way to look, across the bar and she was there. On the far side, with the girl he recognised from the shoot. Sipping a cocktail. In the pub. He shook his head. Bloody cocktails got everywhere. Fancy, expensive and dangerous. Like her.

He slid his gaze back to Steve, and grinned. "Oh, I'm sure." With slow deliberation typed in a reply to the text. *'Who said I was a gentleman?'* And he could have sworn he saw a flush creep along her high cheekbones, even at this distance in the dim light of the bar. He winked, then slid the phone back in his pocket. "Same girl."

"Oh well, happy shagging, mate. Right let's get one more in before last orders shall we?"

"I'm up for it." He glanced over again, caught her watching, but this time she didn't glance away. This time she stared back, and the slow smile that spread over her face could have been a promise or a threat.

Chapter Five

"I've been thinking." Georgie had done a lot of thinking last night after she'd spoken to Rowena. About the land, Jake's accusations. Bumping into him out of the blue. Yes, she was determined, yes, she could be defiant, ignore advice. But she didn't trick people, use them for her own means. She hadn't sought him out. It had just happened. She hadn't even meant to come back here…

"Dangerous."

She shot him a look and carried on talking. "The Drovers is more your style isn't it?"

"Meaning?"

"Well, it's just where you and your mates hang out. So, what were you doing at the club the other night?"

"You mean the type of place where you and your mates hang out?" Jake straightened the haynet and took his time before he looked her way, but he didn't seem needled by the comment.

"Whatever."

"I wasn't at the club." He held up a hand to stop her objection. "I was parked in the car park."

"You were mad at something weren't you? What?"

He shook his head slowly, a rueful grin accompanying the gesture. "Have you come here to work or talk?"

Look, she could have added. He was good to look at. "You

always do that macho burning rubber thing when you're mad don't you?" *And you were doing it again last night.*

"I'll do a macho something if you don't stop trying to wind me up."

"Ooo, sounds good. Promises, promises."

A wry smile teased at the corner of his mouth as he picked up a body brush and curry comb and started a methodical sweep over the mare. Georgie tried not to lick her lips, glad that he seemed immune to the cold and still had on a tight t-shirt, the muscles in his arms stretching and tightening with each firm stroke of the brush.

"Should I be the one doing that?"

"You're doing the next bit." Another firm stroke, then the short jab of soft brush against metal. "Yup, you're right. I was angry, when I met you." A ripple of muscles as the brush came down again on the already shining coat. "I'd spent all frigging day with a colicky horse and we had to let it go. Why do people keep animals if they're going to do that to them?"

"What? What caused it?"

He was putting his whole body behind each stroke with a barely contained frustration. "It was a bag of bones, someone had dumped it in the bottom paddock because they couldn't even be arsed to give it a decent end." He didn't say anything for a moment, kept up the steady brush and scrape in silence. "It was scared stiff and in agony, but the poor sod let us catch it and walk it round." He moved on silent feet to the other side of the mare and Georgie watched the expression on his face as he worked. "Sand colic the vet thought, or bloody worms."

"Maybe someone couldn't afford to keep it."

He glared. "It was well bred, a pretty little thing." He wiped his forearm across his brow and straightened, staring at her for a moment. "More like the kids had got fed up and left it stuck on a bare paddock all summer eating dirt."

Ah, yeah, kids like her. He threw the body brush in her direction and fished a comb out of his pocket. "So, yeah you could say I had a bit of a mood on."

"A bit?" She raised an eyebrow at him, willing the mood to pass.

"You know what pisses me off most?"

"Nope. But I'm sure you're going to tell me."

"People," she could hear the silent 'like you', "who are so fucking well off they forget how to appreciate what they've got." The mare stamped a foot and swished her tail and he ran his hand over her quarters. Slow, soothing. She knew how that hand felt.

"So, what was your excuse?"

She knew what he meant. He'd been mad, needed to let off steam and she'd been there, willing and able. Well, practically begging. "No reason, I just fancied a fuck."

"Not very ladylike."

"I like alliteration." And she'd liked the look of him. If she was honest it had been a mix of adrenalin, fear from being threatened and a sudden need that had hit her when he'd stood like the great protector, a black knight who could banish every memory of the type of evening that needed erasing. You didn't often come across those in a car park. Anywhere.

He was everything the drunken Seb hadn't been. Big, strong, fit and hard with a take it or leave it attitude, and he hadn't cared less who she was or what she had. And he had a motorbike.

"Apparently this horse won't stand still long enough for her ladyship to clamber on, then won't stop." He stroked a hand down the long elegant bay nose before slipping the bridle on and she made a concerted effort to snap out of motorbike thoughts.

"And?"

"And I'm too heavy for her. So you're going to do it."

She'd walked straight into that one hadn't she? For all his defensive crap, Jake mustn't have been able to believe his luck when she'd walked onto the yard and practically waved an 'I'll do anything' sign at him. "And the no stopping bit?"

"Well we both know she will eventually, don't we? But she stops fine when I long rein her." He tightened the girth a notch and nodded to Georgie to open the stable door.

"I haven't got a proper school, so I wouldn't fall off if I were you, that paddock's still hard."

"Gee, ta for the advice. What did you mean yesterday, when you said about it being in your blood? The horses?"

"You can't escape who you are." The horse stood quietly as he checked the tack over, adjusted the stirrups, and cinched the girth up a final hole. From the tight lips he obviously wasn't saying any more on the matter. But she'd find out. Later.

"She flinched when you did that. Maybe she's just cold backed."

"Maybe she's had a crap rider. Here," he waved her over, "I'll give you a leg up and keep her on the lunge."

There was a tiny jitter of nerves playing around in the pit of her stomach, like there always used to be when she went out riding. That not knowing if you'd be bucked off before your bum hit the seat, whether you'd be able to set the pace or just have to go with the flow. Georgie had always been a light rider, not forceful and strong, but even though she was willing to take a chance, risk being out of control, it still scared her at times. Like now.

The warmth of his hand wrapped round her calf and ran headlong over the nerves like a stampeding bull. That fine line between being scared and being turned on. Great, just what she needed before she got on an unstoppable horse. She bit down on her lower lip and tried to stop the pulse of need that was flickering through her body.

He'd hoisted her on before she had time for any more dirty thoughts. The mare stood rock solid, apart from a shiver that shimmied its way through her body from withers to tail. Well that makes two of us girl. She automatically ran a reassuring hand over the warm neck and slowly slid her feet into the irons. Breathed. Sat up straight.

Jake winked. "Scaredy cat."

"Easy for you to say, you're the one that wimped out."

"A humanitarian act."

"Humane, not humanitarian."

"Says the school swot. Okay?"

She nodded and he encouraged the mare into a walk. The ripples of tension travelling right through the leather saddle and into her body. "Stop."

He did immediately, slowed the horse to a stop without a fuss. "And?" Raised an eyebrow.

"I know I'm going to live to regret this, but let's take the saddle off."

Sat bareback on a horse she didn't know, who had a problem with stopping, wasn't Georgie's idea of a good day out. But she had to try it, she went with her instincts, like she always had with her own horse. Which was probably why she'd survived.

They set off again, the choppy stride gradually lengthened with relief and the involuntary shudders faded to an occasional twitch. After three circles Jake grinned and effortlessly called a halt. "Fancy doing a Lady Godiva for me?"

"In your dreams."

She swung her leg over the back of the horse and slid to the ground, and as she touched the ground he was behind her, so close she could feel the warmth of his body.

"I satisfied your dream." His lips were so close to her neck she could almost feel the words seep into her skin. "So maybe it's my turn."

"Who said I was satisfied?"

He chuckled. "The look on your face did, gorgeous." His finger traced a slow path down from her ear, to the point where her neck met her shoulder, along her collarbone to the midpoint. She swallowed, felt the pressure against her skin, the tip of his finger circled and her nipples bruised against the lace of her bra, a warmth building between her thighs.

"You need to sort the mare." Christ, she sounded wanton, where the hell had that husky beg in her voice materialised from?

"I need to sort you." His arm reached up past her, and she watched mesmerised as long fingers with short dirty nails unbuckled the bridle, as he drew it down over the horses head, dropped it at his feet. "So that's the horse sorted." His hands slid over her breasts as the horse ambled off and put her head down to pick at the grass. Firm thumbs circled the hard buds and she closed her eyes, willed the feeling through her body, leant back to stretch her neck, reach out for every last bit of the sensation. "And now it's your turn."

Sharp teeth nipped at her neck and she groaned, tilted her head as his hands travelled down her body, as he popped the button on her jodhpurs effortlessly, reached one hand inside.

He pressed firmly over her covered clit. Shit, that was good, far, far too good. A slow pulse started deep inside her and she knew she was swollen, waiting, wet. One finger reached inside her and she whimpered, she couldn't help it.

"You're as twitchy as that horse."

He slid a second finger in, deeper inside her, sucked on the softness of her neck, his other hand still cradled her breast, strong fingers teasing her nipple.

"And you're hopefully as unstoppa—" Her words were cut off as he pressed that perfect spot that was guaranteed to send her tumbling over the edge. His arm was round her waist, holding her firm as she shot from gentle vibration to explosion in one easy step. And she was still fighting for breath when he eased his grip on her, slid his fingers free, slowly pulled her zip back up.

"Nice to see you tidy up afterwards." There, she nearly sounded normal. When she glanced up he had a dark grin on his face that was almost territorial and the sharp clutch in her stomach was more like fear than pleasure. "And you're not a one trick pony." It still didn't goad him into saying anything, or lighten his features.

Finally, when she was just on the verge of either hitting him or letting go with a spout of verbal diarrhoea, the fixed features relaxed.

"Oh, I'm not a pony Georgina, I'm all grown up," his finger rested lightly under her chin so that she couldn't look away if she wanted to. Not that she wanted to, she was more than a match for his staring games, even if they did leave her a bit overheated like a grill someone had forgotten to switch off. "Just like you."

"So, why didn't you finish the job off, like a real man?" Shit, how did they go from mind bending sex to sparring like it was a natural progression? Georgie knew she had the power to wind people up, but she didn't want to. Not really. She didn't like the antagonism, it was just a game, to get a reaction. But with Jake, she had a horrible feeling that if she let him he'd lead her somewhere far more dangerous.

He chuckled, and the low rumble sped like an express train straight to the still warm, swollen part of her between her legs. "You mean shag you? Having it all handed out on a plate is boring, fighting for it is much more fun."

"Christ, you're infuriating."

This time when he laughed it was the full all on male version and it made her smile. Even though she didn't really want to. Even his damned eyes seemed to join in.

"Come on, I'll give you a coffee."

"No food?"

"I don't eat in the day." Or anything else it seemed. She tried not to pout.

"No food at all, nothing? But I'm hungry."

"So am I darling, hunger is good."

She preferred satisfaction personally.

"And this isn't bed and board, it's just a job." He was laughing at her again.

"Some bloody job, I don't even seem to be getting paid in kind."

"I'd say we get exactly what we deserve." She was almost shocked when his firm lips came down unexpectedly on hers. A short bruising contact that made the riposte on the tip of her tongue head off somewhere else of its own accord. He smelled of sex, shared lust, but she knew he wasn't going to give in whatever she did. She wasn't quite sure if he was paying her back, tormenting her, for threatening to move back here, or whether that primal urge inside her had found its match. Either way, finishing the job he'd started would have been more fun. Maybe he'd decided in his macho way that he could make her rethink by making her desperate for him. Well bollocks to that, two could play at that game.

She didn't move back, stayed where she was, with that few inch gap between their lips. Refused to reach up and touch that perfect mouth, or stroke her own tender aching ones like she wanted to.

"Let's get that coffee then, shall we?"

"Sounds good to me." He didn't move either, the warm breath that accompanied his words drifting over her. Boy, was he smooth. And sexy. "Rowena called me this morning, she wants to see me, us." The way he said it sent a little shiver down her spine. "Now, I wonder what that is all about?"

She licked her suddenly dry lips. "You rang her first."

"I did."

"We could go now."

"We could indeed. I can't wait." The dry tone prickled its way over her skin and for some reason made her suddenly uneasy. Rowena had refused to commit to anything last night, she'd said she couldn't make any decisions until she'd talked to Jake. She owed him that much. And he'd been so cool this morning, as though he hadn't got a care in the world. But he'd already spoken to Rowena, arranged to see her. Exactly what was his game?

***

"You're father sold the land to me several years ago, Georgina."

"But he can't…"

Jake watched the way the colour fled from Georgie's face like she'd seen a ghost and felt a sudden twinge of pain for her which shattered the brief feeling of satisfaction when Rowena had said the words. He'd turned to her feeling a strange triumph and now he felt the victor without the spoils. A complete bastard.

He didn't get why this particular small patch of grass was so important to her, after all she could have whatever she wanted and she already had lots. A fair chunk of the county he'd imagine after growing up watching from afar how the other half lived. But, for some reason there was real grief behind the shocked response. And if it had been anyone else, anywhere else he'd have just said fine, and walked away.

"He can't have sold it. He wouldn't… Why didn't you say so, last night?"

"I'm sorry, but I think maybe he wanted to break all ties with the past, move on. I still don't quite understands why he's kept the house so long, maybe he thought she'd come back."

Georgie was gritting her teeth, the tension invading every inch of her taut body. "She isn't coming back, he doesn't want her to."

"I didn't tell you last night, because I might, and that is just a might mind you, consider selling."

It was Jake's turn to be shocked now, no way would she just sell it from under him. He thought they had a deal, that he could trust her. So much for the thought that money didn't rule the world. "But I need to be fair to both of you. And you can call me an old busybody but I think you've both got some thinking to do. I love having you next door Jake," she reached out and put a hand on his knee, a touch he tried not to shrink from but he could feel every muscle tight in his leg. Recoiling from the rejection to come. "And you're a natural with the horses, but maybe it's time you thought about the future." She drew back, the small clear blue eyes studying him steadily. "Your dad would be proud—"

"I don't give a shit—"

She held up a hand. "Well you should. He was a good man who tried hard to do the right thing, he just took a bad turning and we all make mistakes. Don't we?"

She was looking stern, judgemental and the wisest thing was

obviously to keep his trap shut. "We do, Jake." She answered for him. "You need to make a commitment, not keep dodging the issue. You can't just rent a place on a week by week basis for the rest of your life."

"I can if I choose to live like that."

"No, you can't. How does that make you any better than your father? At least his mistakes were made when he was trying his hardest for you and your mother. He didn't dodge his responsibilities, which is what you're trying to do, he tried to change things. Move on."

"I don't want responsibilities." He regretted saying the words as soon as they came out. It was none of her business, or Georgie's, how he lived his life.

"Well, you have them, each horse you take on is a responsibility. Each client, whether you like it or not. So," she paused, "enough of the lecture, but I have a proposal. I want you to think about raising a deposit and signing a five year agreement for the place. I need security even if you don't." Her gaze softened. "I'm getting older Jake, and I need to think about what's going to happen to this place. The last thing I want to do is sell it off to some property developer, but one day I might have to." She switched her gaze to Georgie. "And you, Georgie. You were such a lovely child, I'm sorry things turned out like they did for you." He watched the pink tinge tiptoe its way over her cheekbones. However much bravado she had, she didn't like to be the centre of attention, didn't want to be commented on. "Being old means I get to finally say what I want." A slow smile spread over her features and Jake felt a pang. He loved Rowena like a mother, even if she was so wrong. "It isn't enough to just want this place on a whimsy, nostalgia, whatever it is. What are you going to do if you buy it?" She paused, but not long, obviously not expecting an answer. "If you want me to consider it then I need to know why, I want a proper business plan off you. Proof that you will stay around and stick at it. I'll say it again, I don't want this place to be sold to developers either now or in a few years' time. I've fought against that for too long to put up with it now. Your father works hard to give you the lifestyle you've had Georgina and you need to grow up a bit and realise that. Now, that doesn't mean you should work for him and live your life how he dictates, but you can't just live a life of rebellion. You need to find your own path." She looked from one to the other. "And stick to it. I don't understand you young people these days, too much wallowing and not enough getting on with it to my mind." She struggled to her feet, grimacing at the arthritis that he knew plagued her. "And this damp weather doesn't help anyone. Right I've finished my old lady rant and I need a cup of tea. You've both got a month, Jake you decide how much you want to stay and if you can raise the proper deposit and sign a long term agreement so this is on a proper footing and an old lady can relax, and Georgina you need to give me a business plan that proves you aren't going to waste the opportunity. Off you both trot now and leave me in peace."

"But—" Georgie was looking at her open mouthed. He wasn't going to say a single word.

Rowena put a hand up and cupped his face briefly. "I've been thinking about this for the past six months or so Jake, since my fall. If you don't want to commit, then you can rent one of the other fields, but I can't promise how long I'll be around." He would have liked to have hated her, a woman he'd trusted letting him down. But he couldn't. It was the closest he was going to get to an apology, but better than he got from most people.

He stuck with a smile, not trusting himself to say anything. She still needed him around, whatever she said, and he'd have put money on it that it would be a long time before she sold up. Yeah, he could have another field. But why should Georgie just walk in and change everything? She didn't need this place, it was a passing whim, but he had a horrible feeling he did. If he walked now he was giving up, throwing away the one thing he'd found worth fighting for, working at.

But this deal wasn't what he'd been expecting at all. And nor had Georgie from the look on her face. He'd never seen her speechless for that long before.

"I'll talk to you both soon." And they were ushered out with an unexpected firmness; the curtain twitching behind them as they walked down the path.

"I always said she was a mad old bat."

He laughed. "Slightly eccentric I'd say." They walked the short distance down the lane side by side. Not quite touching, but striding in time. "So, what's so bad about living the life your father wants you to? Why come back here?"

"Trying to get rid of me? You'll have to do better than that." Her tone was light, but she shoved her hands in her pockets in the slightly defensive way he was getting used to seeing, her shoulders hunched as she thought of an answer.

"Georgie." He paused midstride, put a hand on her arm so that she would stop, look at him. "Don't do this. It's not a game." He never begged, never asked for anything. But he had to ask her.

"You don't understand. I've got to."

Chapter Six

"You know I'd love to go out, but I've got to start this business plan."

"A business plan?" Ella laughed, dumped her bag and sank into the sofa like she planned to stay. "Since when did you plan anything?"

"You'll have to either go away or help."

"Oh, I get it. It's the biker boy's field. Haven't you dropped that yet?"

"It's not his field, it was mine."

"*Was* being the main word here."

"How the hell was I supposed to know he'd be renting it? Anyway, now it's Rowena's and I'm going to buy it."

"Why in God's name would you want to do that?" Ella put her feet up on the coffee table and crossed her arms. "Come on, tell. You've given me the sanitised '*I had an idyllic time there and I have a big plan*' story, now give me the rest. Because I sure as hell don't understand at the moment, and I don't think for one moment anybody else does either."

Georgie slid her laptop onto the table slowly and sat back down. "They used to call me swot at school." *Until it all went wrong.* She put her feet up next to Ella's and studied her polka dot socks.

"Swot, you? But you aren't…"

"Clever? Nope, I was never that bright but I worked. I didn't get on with many of the other kids, they hated me, thought I was stuck up." She leaned her head back, closed her eyes. Maybe she had seemed stuck up, she had been too shy to push herself forward and when she'd joined the school a few months after everyone else they already had friendship groups. And she was the one on the outside, quietly watching. Maybe Alfie had done the right thing, after things had gone wrong, when he'd moved her on to boarding school. Or at least maybe he thought he was doing the right thing. "But I liked the teachers so I did everything they said, all my homework, I'm not smart but I did work hard. I always had my head down, so I was the swot." After all, if you had no friends, what else were you supposed to do all day? "The one thing I really loved was my horse, that stroppy, temperamental black devil kept me sane. And I was with Dad when I was with her."

"You called him Dad."

"Yeah." She wouldn't cry, she just would not get sentimental. "He was dad back then, a proper dad not some stupid jerk." Angry helped. "I wanted to work with horses, teach people to ride. When I was fifteen I was helping kids out with their ponies, giving lessons and stuff." And when I was sixteen it was all over. Horse sold, house gone, the end of the school swot. "That's what I'm going to do now, Ella. Not some stuffy dead-end job like they want me to do."

"It might not be the same now Georgie, things change." Ella had grabbed her hand, and she knew why. She thought she was mad, thought she was just trying to turn the clock back. But she wasn't. "People change, you're a different person now."

"And I'm going to paint. That silly cow stopped me after I got thrown out of college, but Sly said I was good."

"Sly, what kind of a god awful name is that?"

"Sylvester."

"So, was he named after the cat or the actor?"

"A singer." She grinned. "He was conceived at some hippy thing with 'You make me feel' echoing in the background."

"Made someone feel something then."

"Obviously."

"And Sly was?"

"The art teacher who I got caught posing with." Ella raised an eyebrow. "He asked me and another girl to assist him, said it fed his muse."

"A threesome? I bet it fed something."

"Artistic licence I think they call it. Tons better than looking at his etchings." She twiddled her toes. "I think I might call him, I mean maybe I could set up some kind of artistic retreat, run classes or something. I'm sure Sly has loads of contacts."

"Loads of something by the sound of it."

"He's run these retreat things lots of times, he wanted me to go on one and pose—"

"I bet he did."

"He can come and see the place, tell me what to put in the plan."

"What about Jake?"

"What about Jake?"

"Well, he might want to stay there. I mean, it is his place at the moment and he does seem keen."

"He's just trying to rile me, make life difficult." She didn't quite get why he was kicking up such a fuss, despite thinking about it long and hard. Yes, he liked Rowena, but she'd said she'd rent him a field out. And he only had one horse on there. "Jake doesn't want to be tied down to anything or anybody. He keeps making a point of telling me, making sure I get the message and don't get clingy." She grinned to herself. Clingy was the last thing she was these days, take it or leave it worked fine for her. She glanced at Ella. "He doesn't want a mortgage or any kind of commitment."

"Are you sure about that? He doesn't seem the fuss type, more take it or leave it, not just do something to annoy you."

Which was what was niggling her. "Exactly. But he's just trying to prove I can't have what I want. He's got a thing about people with money."

"Ah."

"Thinks I'm a spoiled brat."

"Figures. Posh totty."

"Don't say that, it sounds horrible. He's not bothered about the place though and he will never commit to taking it on."

"Are you sure?" Ella was grinning at her and the flutters of apprehension smacked about a bit harder in her bloodstream. A couple of days ago she'd have said yes without a pause, Jake was a wanderer, a bad boy with no roots, nothing pinning him down. Free. But he'd been angry and shocked at Rowena's proposal. And although he'd been pleasant enough, the band of steel that ran straight through him had never been more evident.

"Yes, yes." If she said it enough it would be true. "He's messing about, he doesn't want it. No way will he go through with it. He doesn't even need a place for what he does."

"Can we call it a day on the business plan and go for a drink then?" Ella had obviously lost interest. "You've got a shitload of ideas, so let's leave it at that eh? I'm sure Sly will be very accommodating if you ask him." She winked and dodged the thump Georgie threw her way. "Come on, stop being boring, it's wine o'clock, girl."

***

He was out. No sign of him, or his motorbike. Which hopefully meant she'd be gone before he got back. She felt a bit like an unwanted intruder, but she had text to ask him if it was okay to pop in and have a poke around. Not that she'd mentioned she was taking someone with her.

And she had got a 'fine' back. It could have been a fine, I don't care, or a fine, if you have to, or a fine, I haven't got much choice have I. She favoured the last one, hence the unwanted intruder feelings.

Sly had been a bit non-committal when she rang him, which

72

she put down to the fact that he probably had his latest shag, sorry muse, either next to him or under him at the time. But he'd rung her back in the early hours, so obviously not a shag who had got to the coveted staying-the-night status, and he'd actually started to sound marginally enthusiastic. Sly didn't do enthusiasm any more than he did fidelity. He was actually in the area the next afternoon he said, before taking the redeye to the States, so he could spare her a couple of hours. As long as she wasn't expecting more, and she gave him a lift to the airport. Treat 'em mean, keep 'em keen was a saying that could have been made for him.

She wasn't expecting more. And she was so glad she hadn't been when she saw him. He'd aged, or maybe she'd just grown up from being an awe inspired student and his god-like status had slipped. It was embarrassing, but she was pretty sure she was staring at him gobsmacked when he walked out of the railway station. Not that it would bother him, Sly liked to be stared at.

Black leather Dr Who coat swinging open, his shoulder length dirty blond hair scraped back into a ponytail to show off beautiful high cheekbones that a sculptor couldn't have bettered. He'd once seemed Byronesque to her, now he was more aged rock star with a slightly dodgy taste in clothes. But he still had it, that certain something. And even though now she could just look at him as an observer, she could see why the teenage Georgie had been drawn in. And hadn't wanted to get out.

He stood for a moment, getting his bearings. And then he spotted her, whipped off the dark sunglasses and his lazy drawl of a gaze took her in from head to toe. The grey eyes looked hazy, he was probably drunk, or at least well oiled. But when he spoke, it was the same familiar voice that had teased and tempted her out of her safety zone, goaded her into painting flamboyantly, caressed her until she practically made a fool of herself trying to catch his attention. And when he winked, it was the same old Sly.

"Well, well little Gina haven't you grown up?" He grabbed her firmly by the shoulders, he probably thought it was a flamboyant gesture, but it bloody hurt. Whether that meant grown up as in filled out, or got fat, or something less catty she wasn't sure. Sly had a sharp tongue on him, he preferred to call it acerbic wit, and in a strange way it appealed to the young naïve girls that he choose to surround himself with. Teaching in a college had served him well. But he had improved her art no end, she had to admit that. Whether it was because of his skill, or the fact she'd put in incredible hours just to get his attention was, she supposed, pretty immaterial. "Lead me to your well, my darling."

Which could have meant anything, maybe it was the horse thing he'd latched on to and leading a horse to water, or maybe her 'well' was a part of her she'd rather not share with him these days. Yes, he was undeniably attractive, she had to admit that. In fact, she had to keep admitting that as she kept sneaking a look at him as they headed towards Marsh Lane. But, seeing him now was like stepping into her past, back into the life she used to have. And sadly, she didn't want to go back there. She sighed, it had been so good while it lasted. So uncomplicated.

The drive to the smallholding was over quickly, which was a bonus seeing as old Sly insisted on laying a hand on her upper thigh, and pressing a soothing thumb into her inner thigh until not squeaking became an ordeal in self-control. He just didn't do it for her any more. Which was a shame.

But the second he stepped out of the car he forgot her. Sly was like that, his passion flipped between carnal and earthly, but at the root of it all was a deep commitment to beauty, whatever form it took. Which, she supposed, was part of his appeal. She'd purposefully killed the engine just short of the barn, a high point from which the countryside spread out below, framed by the oak tree in all its autumn glory. Whether your heart was with the abstract or convention, this view held the kind of promise you couldn't ignore.

Georgie let him stand, silent, for as long as it took. Sly was fast, mercurial most of the time. Demanding and wearing, generous and greedy, having him silent was a gift she wasn't going to waste. When he finally spun to look at her, coat billowing, there was pure greed shining in those flinty eyes.

"*While barred clouds bloom the soft-dying day, And touch the stubble-plains with rosy hue.*"

"Sorry?" Georgie raised an eyebrow as he peered down his aquiline nose.

"Keats. *Season of mists and mellow fruitfulness, Close bosom-friend of the maturing sun.* Although mellow death is how I like to think of it. A bastard to capture, but so rewarding if you manage it." The corner of his generous mouth curled. "Just like you."

What the heck was he on about now? She wasn't that keen on the look in his eye, over-zealous was probably how she'd think of it. Apparently now his artistic nature had been teased, some other part of him had been as well.

"Why don't you show me your inner sanctum?"

Like hell she would. She was, she supposed, still attracted to him in some weird way. Maybe it was the passion that seeped out of every pore, the expression of pure want. Sly had the ego of a rock star, which was no wonder really, the way his students fell beneath him before he even asked. And he had that dangerous, forbidden aura about him, which was probably what had appealed to her in the first place. But now he was no longer forbidden, now he was no longer the mentor, the god-like figure of authority, now he was just a man who really could do with a good haircut and a smartening up. God, she was starting to sound like Carol, any second now she'd be telling him he needed to settle down and write a five year plan.

She smiled and she saw it in his eyes. That recognition. He took her hand and linked it through his arm and past lover faded to friend. Sly would never pursue what he knew he couldn't attain, the challenge only appealed when he knew he could win the race. The lust hadn't faded away, it had been extinguished, a single brushstroke wiping it away forever. Sly was no hesitant artist who dabbled and changed, he attacked the canvas, unforgiving and bold. Just like he'd attacked her.

He dropped a light kiss on the top of her head. "Show me."

They walked in silence the short distance to the barn and the instant they stepped inside his hand slipped away as he gazed upwards into the darkness.

"A perfect retreat, my dear." He slowly turned, taking in every inch of the barn with an artist's eye that placed every detail, saw every sweep of light and shade. The smile that broke through this time was genuine, not his moody genius look, as he placed one hand either side of her face and stared straight into her eyes. "Let me count the ways I took thee."

She sighed. "You've gone very poetic, except even I know that's a serious misquote."

"Being with you makes me that way."

"I bet it does." Neither of them had heard him approach, but he was stood, framed in the barn entrance, the sunlight wrapped around him. A tall defiant figure, arms folded, legs hip width. Jake. The soft words reaching out to them in the cavernous space.

"Oh, it does." Sly's voice was soft, but carried with the expertise of a lecturer, and the gentle kiss he dropped on her mouth was executed with the skill of an experienced lover. Then he slowly let his hands fall to his sides.

Georgie cringed, that was all she needed. Mr Judgemental. "You're back." That's it girl, state the obvious.

"Don't let me disturb you."

"We won't." God, she wished he'd caught her in a clinch or something, anything. Well not anything.

Sly winked at her, kissed her again on the nose this time, his eyes twinkling. "Ah, so this is the obstacle in the way of our plans."

Okay, Jake hadn't needed to catch her doing anything, Sly was perfectly capable of winding a man up as effectively as he was of wooing a woman. And now he'd walked up to Jake and was studying him like a still life. Guaranteed to irritate.

"It's been wonderful, darling." He turned the slightest degree in her direction, but his attention was still on Jake. "I'd have stayed longer, hopefully I will next time? A week or two?" Yup, he was turning the handle, putting on the pressure. "Let's talk in the car shall we?"

She could feel the seethe as she walked past Jake, but still didn't expect it when he reached out and stopped her, strong fingers curled around her upper arm. Bad habit.

"Who the hell is that?"

"Part of my business plan."

"Well it's a pretty fucked up business. What do you want with someone like that?"

"You sound just like my father."

"Has it ever occurred to you that sometimes he might have a point?"

"Has it never occurred to you that I might actually know what I'm doing?"

"That man's a waster, and he's old." She could almost hear the 'too old for you'.

"For your information," okay she hadn't planned on telling him anything, not yet, not until she had a clear idea in her own head, "he's an artist." His upper lip was heading for a sneer. "An acclaimed artist, and he was my tutor."

"Your tutor? Looks like he still wants to give you a lesson or two."

"Bastard." She lashed out with her free hand, but it wasn't free for long. Caught effortlessly before she had the satisfaction of contact.

"Well, come on; you're not an artist."

She knew she was scowling at him, every muscle in her face competing to show just how angry she was.

"You are?" The pressure around her arm eased. "I didn't—"

"You don't know anything about me, Jake Harcourt. Now let go, Sly's got a 'plane to catch."

"Sly?" The short laugh said it all.

Here we go again. She wasn't even going to grace that with a response.

He suddenly sobered, let go of her completely. "I just don't like the look of him." His arm dropped to his side.

"You don't say."

"Georgie, the man…" He tailed off. "It's none of my business."

"Got it in one."

What was the point in even slapping him? He hated her, he thought she was incapable, and he didn't really care anyway. Just like Alfie. Her father had hated Sly on sight. Alfie was as traditional as they came, and he distrusted any man with long hair and artistic tendencies. As far as he was concerned, Sly needed a proper job. He wasn't a proper man. And when he'd found out he was shagging his young daughter it confirmed every bigoted belief he held dear.

Georgie closed her eyes briefly. That had been one hell of an explosion that she never, ever wanted to see repeated in her life. It had rivalled the one when her mother had walked out, but this time the fury had been directed straight at her. And now Jake was headed to exactly the same place.

"Just," he obviously wasn't going to let up, she waited; "oh forget it, just do exactly what you want, like you always do."

"Finished? I need to go, he's got a 'plane to catch."

"So you said. Well let's hope he misses the one back."

Chapter Seven

"You're wasting your time. Nobody in."

The motorbike had headed straight to her house like it was a homing pigeon and even Jake's first rap had been angry, by the time he'd progressed to what must have been the sixth or seventh attempt at raising her he'd been close to riding up the steps and ramming the bloody door at 50 mph.

Now, as the soft tone broke through his impatience he spun round expecting to be furious. But oddly, he wasn't. He was pleased to see her. "You are. You're in."

"Nope, not my front door anymore."

"It is, I dropped you—"

"I've been demoted to the apartment." She nodded to the right. "But I heard the bike."

"You didn't answer your 'phone."

"I put it on mute, it was annoying me."

He'd wanted answers the moment she walked out on him, with her aged hippy of an artist, so he'd rung. No answer. And with each unanswered call his gut had twisted tighter and his need to know had escalated until he knew he was being ridiculous. Acting out of character. But when it had hit 9pm he'd decided he had a choice. Go and find her, or get drunk. He'd opted for the first.

I mean, just who was the guy? Friend, lover? The way he'd had his hands on her, the way he'd kissed her like he was staking some kind of claim, like some stud marking his territory, the way she'd let him. That wasn't about casual acquaintances. That was the way lovers behaved. Lovers with unfinished business.

Jake could feel the muscles in his shoulders curl up a bit tighter. Why would a girl like Georgie let someone like that into her life? A dead-end idiot who knew a good thing when he saw it. Rich, young, sexy. He didn't know what bothered him more, the fact that Georgie seemed happy to go along with it, or the fact that he wanted to stop it. He needed to know if the guy was on his plane, and he needed to know exactly why Georgie had walked into his life and seemed set on turning it upside down and inside out. If he was going to get fucked, he wanted to know why.

She'd taken her mobile out of her pocket and was waving it at him.

"See, no sound." She glanced at the display. "Oh, yeah, you have been trying to get hold of me." Raised an eyebrow, part quizzical, part mischief. "What it is to be popular." But the tone was dry.

He sighed with exasperation. Yeah, he knew that feeling, when he could have thrown his mobile in a bucket of water. But she'd just been avoiding *him*, not the rest of the world. "You can't just ignore me." Her raised eyebrow said she could. "We had a deal."

"A deal, it doesn't mean you own me, I just said I'd give you a hand when I could. And today I couldn't."

"Why not? Busy with your artist friend?"

"I told you, he was catching a plane. Not that it's any of your business."

"Maybe not." Normally this was the part when he walked. But she'd made it his business, when she'd brought the man onto the land. His land. "So you weren't," he paused, "tied up with him?"

Her brown gaze met his, then she glanced down at her fingers, then back up. "A bit tricky with that many miles between us."

"Georgie."

She sighed. "Well, he did text when he landed, and he did ask me to send some info to him." She shrugged. "That's all. We're working on something together, if you must know. Now, can we just forget him?"

"Fine, it's nothing to do with me."

"And I had other stuff to do, I have got a life you know."

"What are you doing here?" He leant back against his bike, a slightly sullen, hurt expression sat on her features and it shouldn't have been there. It should be him that was angry, not her.

"I live here."

"Georgie."

"Okay." Her long legs covered the distance between them and she flung one effortlessly over the bike, leant forward and rested her forehead on her slim hands. "Sorry." The muffled word came out with an effort then she slowly straightened and stared at him.

"How come you're not in the main house?" One step at a time, slowly or she'd be backing off.

"Alfie put it out on long term rent after we moved." She slowly stroked along the engine, her pale fingers and scarlet nails a sharp contrast against the black. Black and colour, hard and oh so soft. "But he sorted the apartment for me when I said I wanted to come back." She took a deep breath, but the dark gaze never wavered from his face. "They'd have done anything to get me out of their hair for a while, I'm a bad influence on their sweet little kids." The laugh was humourless.

"I bet." He felt an urge to lean forward, kiss her, but resisted.

"They've tried to keep as a big a distance between us as they can." She shrugged. "Hence the boarding school, finishing school, blah, blah, blah."

"Art college?"

"Yup, Art college."

He could almost see the defensive cloak wrap around her as though she was expecting an attack. "But?"

"But I'm still supposed to be under their control, do exactly what they want."

Which explained the bad behaviour he supposed, defiance at a distance. "And what do they want, Georgie? Is it really that bad?"

"Oh yeah, now they've paid for me to look the part I'm supposed to serve them, worse than the bloody Stepford Wives."

He couldn't help it, he laughed. "I'd love to see a submissive version of you."

"Not going to happen."

"Not even if I tie you down?" He couldn't help himself, even though he'd sworn to himself that he'd keep his hands off her for once.

"I envied you at school, you know." She turned her head to look at him, those big dark eyes wide with the little girl lost look she'd had after they'd had sex on his bike. The look he hadn't been able to shake when he'd lain in bed at night.

"Me? Now there's a turn up."

"You always did exactly what you wanted." She was staring at him, through him, as though she was looking into the past.

"Not always a good thing."

"But you had fun."

"Are you having fun? Winding your dad up, are you really doing what you want?"

"It's better than doing what he wants."

"So you keep saying, but I'm not convinced."

She huffed and changed tack. "Why are you here, Jake?"

"I asked first." He'd asked and still not got any answers, but he would. "You wouldn't answer my calls." He slid down, his back against the bike, sat on the gravel which was safer than being so close to her. Until she joined him.

She sighed. "I swear Alfie has people watching me, he just knew Sly was here. I'm sure he did. He's got this sixth sense for when I'm doing something he might not like, so he kept bothering me and asking me what I was doing."

"Ah, so that's why you ditched the phone."

"Yup."

"I don't blame him as far as that character goes."

"You don't know him. He's nice."

"Yeah, sure."

"And he's a brilliant artist, he—"

"I thought we weren't talking about him?"

"What happened to the bad boy who did whatever he liked?" She was grinning at him, teasing, sending a rush of blood southwards.

"Is that what you thought I was? Not just a teenager pissed off with the world?"

"You once told me to lighten up and go get what I wanted, rather than just watching and waiting."

"Did I?" He remembered. It wasn't often he'd dared stop and speak to her, but she'd looked so sad that day. Impossible to ignore, as she'd watched him from under that big fringe, stared with those dark solemn eyes.

She nodded.

"And did you?"

"I asked you if that was what you did, do you remember what you said?"

He remembered, it was like a video tape he could replay at will. Her soft question had needled him. That genuine interest, which he knew had to be from her own desperate need, not because she cared. It had scared him.

"You said," she played with the gravel, letting it drop from her fingers back to the ground, "you needed fuck all. Wanting was for morons. All you were bothered about was living for the moment."

"That was a long time ago."

"I was still hoping you'd be that bad boy." She grinned. "You're turning into a bit of a disappointment, mister boring and sensible."

"You aren't," he reached out, brushed her hair back behind her ear, and the pure softness of her skin beneath his fingertips tightened his throat, "a disappointment." He leant forward and that unique mix of soap, perfume and something that was just her worked its magic on his body. "The good girl who quietly watched."

"And learned." She gasped as his lips found her neck and then she was scrabbling to her feet. Hell. "Not here." There was a tremble in the words, but he knew that tremor, the one that came from deep inside. Want. Need. She was stepping back, pulling at his hand, leading him round to the side of the house. Through a door he barely noticed.

It was an automatic reaction to pin her hands ups above her head, one of his hands easily holding both slim wrists. He slowly stroked down her body, taking in each gentle curve. "He has gone, hasn't he?"

"Yes." She breathed out the word, ran her tongue over full lips. "Did you—"

"He was only here an hour. Please—"

"What happened between you and him?" He watched his thumb as he traced a circle round her hardening nipple, felt the nub firm underneath her thin top. Watched as her breasts rose and fell with each breath.

"It was a long time ago. Jake don't—"

"I need to know. Is he back to stay?" The dip of her waist was warm against his palm, her skin so soft as he slipped his hand under the top, her whimper sending a new rush of blood to his already swollen cock. "Georgie?"

She shifted her weight, leaned into his touch, her thighs parting. "I need his help."

It had to be disappointment, it couldn't be anything else, the hollow that opened up deep inside him. "Then you don't need mine." He let his hand drop away from the tempting warmth.

"Jake."

He shook his head. "Using your money is one thing, but." He let his gaze drift over the perfect body and he couldn't say it. The Georgie he knew wouldn't have slept her way to a solution, the Georgie he'd wanted back then and wanted even more now.

"Jake."

"No." He let go of her wrists, shoved his hand slowly, deep into his pocket. He'd sort it out, he'd raise the money Rowena wanted, and if he couldn't he'd walk. Far, far away from all of this. But until then Georgie Hampton and her grubby little artist weren't laying a foot on his land. Seeing them together once had been bad enough, knowing she was going back for a repeat performance left an emptiness he couldn't label.

"Wait, what about our deal?"

"I don't do deals with people I—" Don't trust? Don't respect? Or just can't bear to be with any longer? He didn't know which, and he didn't want to voice any of them. He stepped back. Leaving would be a good idea, like right now. Before he let rip and said something he'd regret.

"Jake you've got to listen to me." She was running behind him, tugging at his arm, but he just kept straight on going. Got on his bike, tried to ignore the hand grabbing at his helmet as he went to put it on, the tear streaked face. The tears stopped him dead. She'd not made a sound, so he knew they were real.

"I don't want to hear it."

"Please, please just listen."

He stared at the slim hand resting on his helmet, long elegant fingers, nails chipped from working with the horses. "I used to admire you, you know."

Georgie stopped dead, let go of the helmet she was clutching like it was a lifeline. Nobody admired her. Oh yeah, some people would like her for her money, but that was it. "I came back here, Jake because I didn't know where else to go."

He put the helmet down in front of her, his gaze fixed on it.

"Carol hates any reminder of Dad's old life, and I'm a bloody big reminder. I can't do anything right, I'm the devil's spawn." She knew the laugh was a bit maniacal, but she couldn't help it. "I didn't come back here to ruin your life Jake. I came back for some space, some time to think. But when I saw you it reminded me, then that stupid patch of land reminded me even more. I should go, I don't belong here now, you're right."

"What did it remind you?" His voice still had a hard edge to it, unrelenting. But he wasn't moving. He was giving her a chance. One chance.

"I'd forgotten what it was like before Mum left. It all happened so fast, the packing up, the leaving. I'd even forgotten what Dad used to be like." She shoved her hands in her pockets, she mustn't sound sorry for herself. She had to tell it like it was. "They weren't nasty to me or anything, but they sent me away to school and I hated it. I was homesick and I thought that I'd never see them again." She'd not really thought of it properly, but looking back she could see now how scared she'd been, scared of being left alone. If she was honest, Carol had never been anything but kind – in her own way. But she'd been insistent. Georgina had to stay at the school, and everything would be fine. Except it hadn't been fine, because all she could think of was getting home. Getting home and checking that her father hadn't left her. That the whole family had sold up and moved away without even letting her know. In her mind it had been Carol's fault. Not her mother's for leaving her in the first place, but Carol who was going to take her father from her in exactly the same way another man had taken her mother. And they didn't understand, didn't know she was scared. No one knew, not even her. "I reckon I was bad just so I'd get expelled, then I could go home. I think maybe I thought if I didn't then they'd just leave too." Her mother had left, just like that, one day there then next day gone. What was there to stop Alfie and Carol doing the same? "I got crap grades, but I got in at Art college, which was great."

"Until you met the wonderful Sly." Bitter did just not cover the tone of his voice.

"It was just a bit of fun that went too far, but I got thrown out when a group of students came into the room we were, erm, posing in."

"You were having an orgy in a classroom?" He looked at her

then, for the first time.

"Not exactly an orgy, just the three of us. Anyway, after that they just wanted to force me to work for them."

"Doing?"

"They just want me to look pretty and entertain their clients like some upmarket hooker." She sighed, or maybe it was all they could think of that she could do. After all, that was how Carol had met Alfie. Working for him. Maybe to her it looked a good prospect, not the boring trap of tedium that Georgie saw it.

Jake raised an eyebrow, so she ignored that bit. If she lost her temper now, something told her he'd walk. And she didn't want him to walk. Even if he was an over opinionated arrogant bossy boots. "It's boring and pointless, well it's got a point for them like I do the dirty work and get people interested in throwing money their way. And then do you know what they want?" He just looked, but at least he was still there.

"I'm sure you're going to tell me."

"They want to set me up with some stupid city wanker so I'm out of their hair and bored out of my brain for the rest of my life."

"Maybe they just want you to settle down a bit."

Which had too much of a ring of truth about it for her to feel comfortable. "Oh yeah, I'm sure if they still could they'd shove me on a boat and send me to Australia."

He laughed, and strangely enough it didn't get her back up. It made her smile. "Maybe they're worried about you, Georgie. Why not join the family firm? You'd be set up and you could still have fun, do your own thing."

"No way."

"I don't get why you want to make life difficult, why you have to set off on this cock-eyed project."

"It isn't cock-eyed. I want to do my own thing. I can make this work, do it for myself, I'm not making if difficult."

"From where I'm standing you—"

"You're sitting, it's different."

"Funny. Come here." He leaned her way, put a hand on her waist, pulled her closer with one strong arm until she was close enough to kiss him.

"You don't need to do this to prove anything."

"I do. I'm sorry, Jake you don't understand, but I do."

"It won't bring your mum back."

"My mum was never part of all that."

"You can't turn the clock back, it won't change you and your dad, only talking to him will do that."

"Says the man who never talks to his parents."

"That's different."

"Oh, yeah sure, it would be. I'm not trying to turn the clock back. I'm..." she could feel her brow wrinkling as she struggled to find the right words, "I'm going back to the point where it went wrong, but this time I'm going to do it differently."

"And what about me?" His voice was so soft it cut straight through her.

"Maybe, maybe we could, I mean you might not want to, but maybe we could sort something out together?" Okay, another stupid idea straight out of her mouth, bypassing the brain.

"I'm not sure that would ever work, we're different."

"Be my plus one at the party and then you might understand." Oh, God. She shouldn't have said that.

"Plus one? What the hell is one of those?"

"Come with me, you know, be my partner for the night."

"Sod off, I'm not Richard Gere you know."

"Nope, he was a gentleman. Please?"

He sighed. "What party?"

"The very early Valentine's Ball my cow of a step-mother is organising. I really don't want to go and see them all, but Alfie won't drop it."

"Not really a good idea, is it?"

"I'm not going if you don't."

"Childish."

"Come, then you might get why this is important to me. I know you still won't think I should do it, but I just thought…"

"I'll think about it."

"Can I come and help you tomorrow?"

"I'll think about that too." His lips brushed hers, dry, tempting. "But your artist isn't welcome. Right?"

"But—"

"No buts, Georgina. Except maybe this one." A firm hand landed on her left buttock. Warm. Familiar. Pulse quickening.

She swallowed hard. "Can we kiss and make up?"

"You always have to push your luck don't you?" She didn't get to answer, he pulled her in tight with the hand that was still on her waist, and then his other hand was rough against her face, his fingers threading through her hair, holding her still as his mouth came over hers.

Kisses weren't supposed to make you dizzy with sexual urges, but this one made her whole body spring to alert. Her lips were parting while she was still trying to think of a response, his tongue firm against hers, challenging her to respond. So she did, sucking him eagerly, drawing him in deeper. He groaned, pulled her head back roughly and dragged his mouth from hers, the heat of his breath scorching a path down her neck that set up a chain of goose-bumps down her arms, her breasts, setting up a tingling deep down in her stomach, lower between her thighs. His teeth scraped up her neck and she clutched his leather covered arms, willing him not to stop.

His hand was hot against her as he reached under the short skirt, tugged the thick black tights down. She kicked a boot off, wobbled as she pulled a foot free, as he unzipped his jeans, pulled his cock free.

He never shifted from the seat of his bike, instead he pulled her astride him, held her above him then slowly lowered her, nudging her knickers to one side, groaning as her body sheathed him. Kicked the bike back off its stand.

"Shit you're wet, you are such a bad girl." It was his hands that guided her, that raised and lowered her, his firm hands tight around her hips. She couldn't have moved if she'd wanted to. Skirt rucked up around her waist, one leg still covered with her thick wool tights and scruffy boot, the other naked and the contrast turned her on.

"Rub yourself." His voice cracked, harsh and demanding and she reached a hand between them, circled a clit that was already swollen, slipped one finger inside herself, rubbing against his hardness. His thighs trembled under her, wound taut, holding the bike steady. And the pressure as he pulled her down was all she needed and as the first ripples spread, she watched the grimace of control on his face, reached out for him as he lifted her then pulled her back down hard against him, pressed her mouth against his, desperate to taste him as her body shook with need. She was close, so close. "Come for me, Georgie." It was a gruff command and a plea, wrapped in one. A kind of lust and want reaching out to her and it tipped her over that edge, urgent spasms rippling out through her body as his heat filled her.

She was still trembling, legs turned to something closer to blancmange than jelly when he eased his grip on her hips, rocked the bike. She yelped, grabbed at his shoulders and he laughed. A deep down belly laugh that didn't help her regain control one bit. "Good job the neighbours haven't got back yet."

She ran her tongue over her parched lips. "Darling Daddy would not be pleased."

"And, how about his darling daughter?"

"His darling daughter is very pleased thank you."

He smiled, the first real smile she'd seen on his face that day. "You're impossible." Then he gently lifted her off him and stood her back at the side of the bike, shaking his head as he looked her up and down. "Totally impossible." He zipped up, pulled his helmet on. And kicked the bike into action.

"There isn't anything going on between me and Sly." With the roar of the bike she didn't think he'd heard her, but she needed to say it. He slowly swept the motorbike in a large circle, total control, gave a final shake of his head then headed towards the gate.

Georgie glanced down. What was happening to her? She liked designer clothes and high heels and she was stood semi clothed on the driveway, one boot on and one boot off with sopping knickers. She looked back up and he was still at the bottom of the drive, and she knew he was staring, even though his helmet visor shaded his eyes.

She smiled, and then she laughed. She couldn't help it. And she was still laughing as he revved the bike up, spinning gravel and kicking out fumes as he did a wheelie out of the gates.

Chapter Eight

"Fuck." Georgie sat on the loo seat with her head in her hands and considered all the things she could do. Like commit suicide, leave the country… drink a bottle of gin. Funny wasn't it, how every time she thought she'd got a plan sorted, life karate-chopped it dead? Not so funny.

She straightened up. The other option was go to the frigging party and drop the all-time clanger of her life. Or she could just keep her mouth zipped until she thought of a better idea. She pulled herself up, clammy palms against the cool ceramic of the wash basin and stared at her reflection. She still looked the same, but inside she felt like she'd just leapt off a cliff and was free falling like an autumn leaf, spinning into oblivion.

Get a grip girl. She screwed up her mouth. You're not unique, it happens all the time. *But not to me.* People sort it. You can sort it. It might not even be true. But it was, she knew it was.

Her periods had always been regular, bang on time from the day they'd started. Within an hour. The only predictable thing in her life. And when she'd been late, she'd actually been convinced she had got the dates wrong. Her body didn't do things like this to her.

And then she'd felt queasy at the smell of a large brandy and she knew. Brandy had always smelled good, a heady smell that hit the back of her throat with a satisfying heat even before she took a sip. Her body was seriously doing a u-turn on her and there was only one possible reason.

She was pregnant.

Christ, she hoped she didn't go off chocolate as well. That really would be the pits. And what about sex? Or wasn't being pregnant supposed to make you more randy? She certainly hadn't noticed her libido take a nose dive, even if everything else had.

She needed a plan, and the sooner the better. She'd never craved for kids, no way did she want a baby in her life. She'd seen the devastating effect they could have. If her mother hadn't been pregnant she wouldn't have walked off with her toy boy, and she was convinced that if Carol hadn't entered a breeding programme like an eager stud mare, then Alfie would still be the dad she used to love. Which reminded her…

Party. She had to concentrate on the party. She had to get changed, slap on a thick layer of make-up and pretend she was the same Georgie she'd always been, not the one with the bottomless pit opening up in front of her. And she had to go with Jake. Standing him up might be a better idea, she could tell him he'd been uninvited, or it had been cancelled – no, he'd expect them to go out somewhere else then. And she'd actually been looking forward to going out with him, well, him accompanying her. Bugger.

He was a quick fling, nothing more, what was happening to her? She felt like collapsing on the bed and putting her head in her hands again. Since when had Jake been so important in her life? Since she'd woken up with a smile on her face looking forward to working the horses with him. Since she realised she missed him when they had days apart, days when she drifted not quite sure what to do. Picking up her phone to text him, then realising she'd already sent ten that morning already.

He was a friend. That was all. They'd got friendly. Shared a sense of humour and a love of horses. Simple.

And now she was pretty sure they were about to share a hell of a lot more. Oh hell, what was she going to do?

By the time she'd pulled herself together there wasn't much time to do anything else but shrug herself into the first little black dress she found in the wardrobe. And she was just peeling on black stockings when the doorbell went – and so did the stockings, an almighty ladder from knee to mid-thigh. She gave a small scream of frustration, tugged them off and threw them across the room. The bell went again, this time he'd obviously decided to keep his finger on it. Okay, okay keep your hair on. And again in sharp bursts that pierced straight through her head and out the other side. She so wasn't up to this tonight.

Grabbing her stilettos she stomped her way to the door, undecided whether to try a withering look and sarcastic comment or to pull the big girl pants on and admit the whole disaster of her life was down to her and her alone, and not take it out on anyone else.

He was stood finger poised over the doorbell. But she wasn't really bothered about that any more. Devastating. And not in a 'I'm devastated because I've just found out your baby is growing inside me, and we're so not suited, and I so don't want a baby' kind of devastated. No. Deva-sta-ting. Red hot, grab me while you can, oozing sexuality in a barely covered layer of respectability kind of devastating.

She'd not seen him suited and booted before, she hadn't even been able to imagine it, well it had never occurred to her. Jake was leathers and boots, torn jeans and ripped t-shirts, earthy and dirty. Shag on a motorbike sexy. This Jake was ten times more dangerous, her nipples had gone on red alert and the turmoil in her stomach had been suspended.

There was a good chance her mouth was hanging open, and more than a chance that her knickers were damp given the tingling at the top of her thighs and the little urgent pulse between them. Bye 'bye party, hello bed.

"Ready?" He lifted an eyebrow, dark eyes taking her in from tip to toe in a way that made her heat up from the inside out like a halogen hob.

"Shoes." She tore her gaze away, realising that she was giving him as much of a once over as he was giving her. "Bare feet are so not in the look right now. Unless, you'd like to…?"

The laugh was throaty and dirty, then he wrapped an arm round her waist and pulled her up tight against his body. A body that had a very firm bulge in exactly the right place. He moved in, but his lips didn't meet hers, they homed in on her neck. That sensitive spot behind her ear, where her hairline stopped. His warm tongue traced a path down towards her collarbone and she groaned, squeezed her thighs tighter together, and pressed her hips against his so she could rub against his erection. He gently sucked, teeth nipping at her skin and now her knickers were definitely damp, more than damp. She couldn't help it, she lifted a leg, wrapped it around his firm body, shivered as the warmth of his hand drifted down to cradle her bottom.

"You," he was gazing into her eyes, firm dry lips brushing over hers, "are so rude." Strong white teeth tugged at her lower lip as his firm fingers slid between her thighs, stroked over the thin fabric of her panties. "And so wet." One finger slipped under the fabric and she all but whimpered, it nudged between her swollen lips and she gave up on the idea of trying to answer back, her breath was coming too short and all she wanted to concentrate on was those fingers. "We're going to be late for the party." His breath whispered over her ear, sending a rash of goose bumps down her neck and arms.

"We could skip it." But even as her pussy was clutching at his fingers, he was easing away from her. He smiled, slow and lazy, put his hands on her hips and held her at arm's length. Which wasn't where she wanted to be.

"No way, you're not wimping out."

"I'm not a wimp."

"Well I'm quite looking forward to seeing how the other half lives."

"The other half?" She laughed. Annoyed he'd stopped, pleased he still had hold of her. "This is going to be so stuffy and boring you know. A shag would be better?" Always worth one last try.

"The shag is the after dinner finale."

"Spoilsport."

"You got it, and you will get it later, promise." He kissed the tip of her nose and she felt stupidly happy. "Shoes."

***

"So, are you going to introduce me as the bad guy who shags you on his motorbike?"

She was staring at the big door like it was the gate to hell. "No, I've got a better idea. I'm going to introduce you as Richard, Richard Gere." She grinned that grin that never failed to fill him with the urge to get her in a dark corner, even though there was still a trace of that queasiness lurking deep down in her eyes. He wanted to say they didn't have to go in, but he was going to damned well keep that to himself. Hell, he had actually wanted to wrap his arms round her and do something that would make them both a lot happier, but he'd resisted the urge.

"Ha, very funny. Why do you keep calling this a Valentine's Ball? Even I know it's three months early."

"It's a pre Valentine's Ball." Her tone of voice said, *'weren't you listening?'* but it sounded too weird for him. "And it's not me that's called it that, it's her." The tension was building up in her voice.

"Yeah, so you said, but..."

"She calls it that because she's stupid. It's the anniversary of her and Alfie meeting." She made a motion of two fingers down her throat and he laughed, even though he was trying not it. "Puke making, but it gets worse, they got hitched on Valentine's Day."

"He's a quick mover." Bravado was coming out of her mouth, but he couldn't miss the hurt shining in her eyes.

"She is, more like. Once she'd got her claws in." She was glaring at him, as though she was expecting him to say something. So he shrugged. The glare turned to a wary look. "You don't know her."

"I might do soon."

"So she insists on having this stupid party and calling it a Pre Valentine Ball so she can 'keep him to herself on Valentine's Day', yucky."

"I take it you don't approve of Valentine's Day and being romantic then?"

"Got it in one. And why the fuck would you bring it up before Christmas if you weren't just attention grabbing? Valentine's Ball my arse. Why can't they just have a Christmas party like everyone else?"

"Maybe it's true love?"

"And I'm a nun. Love is just another bloody four letter word."

He laughed at her indignation and she actually grinned. "So why did we come?"

"He keeps pestering, and I know it will annoy her."

"Not nice."

She shrugged, but the look on her face was more little girl lost, than bitchy party pooper. He resisted the urge to put his arm round her. "If I go in there with you, then you behave. Okay?" But he had a feeling she would anyway, something was different about Georgie these days. She seemed softer around the edges, more like the old Georgina. And even the Carol jibes had lost their edge, as though even she wasn't convinced that her step-mother was quite the wicked witch she'd once portrayed her. "Okay?"

"God, you are so bossy, and," she paused, that taunting glimmer in her eye, "boring."

"I didn't come here to be just something else to throw in your dad's face, Georgina. I told you, I'm not going to be used." He let his gaze drift over her, he wasn't going to rise to the taunt, but he wasn't going to let it go. "Boring, eh?"

"I'm not trying to use you." She pouted. Even more shaggable. "Maybe abuse you later." Raised those arched eyebrows a little bit higher and all but winked.

Jake shook his head and wondered for the hundredth time why he'd agreed to this. There were two obvious answers, one the urge to shag her senseless still hadn't diminished one iota, and the other was that she was still a complete mystery to him. If he was going to divert her from her ludicrous plan to claim her field back, then he had to know why she was so keen to have it in the first place. The thought of speaking to her father had crossed his mind, briefly, but he was still ashamed it had even occurred to him. She had enough issues with her family, without him adding to them.

He was happy the way things were, he hadn't wanted to commit to staying, but he didn't want to leave either. Which Rowena knew, and was playing on. And Georgie's idea to work together was the worst yet. She'd get fed up of playing ponies at some point and sell up, leaving him in the lurch, or even before that happened there was a good chance that the lust would take a nosedive and he'd want to move on. And then what? He didn't want to get tied to the land, and he definitely didn't want to get tied to a woman. Even a very sexy one like the girl stood in front of him.

"Get the doorbell rung, girl. No after dinner treats until we've had the main course."

She stuck her tongue out, but reached out to ring the bell with one hand, and reached for him with the other.

***

Jake recognised Alfie the moment he walked across the room. Tall and slim, an unmistakeable air of authority which came from wealth and education, just like Georgie. She had obviously got the delicate beauty, the refinement and her air of innocence and doubts from her mother – but the rest came from Dad. And Jake guessed that the stubborn side of her nature came from her father, mixed with a naughtiness from her mother. Which added up to one hell of a dangerous package.

Carol was nothing like he'd imagined. Warm, welcoming, a mother figure and he could see without trying that she would have been at a loss when it came to dealing with the difficult teenager that Georgie was turning into when they'd first met. They were opposites, in a love match it might have worked, in the land of step-parent, defiant daughter there was no way.

Her eyes darted anxiously from Jake to Georgie, then up to Alfie. But when he glanced at Alfie himself, the steady gaze was fixed firmly, no wavering there. And it was fixed on him.

"You're Harcourt's son aren't you?"

He was surprised the man had recognised a nobody like him, even more surprised that there didn't seem to be judgement in the tone. Early days though.

He nodded. "I am. Jake."

"Pleased to meet you again." The handshake was firm, just like he'd expected. But he hadn't expected the hand on his shoulder. "It's been a long time. A lot of water under the bridge, eh?"

"You could say that." Any minute now it would be dredged up. The fall from grace.

"I liked your father, he was a good man, could sell ice to the Eskimos that one." He chuckled, but there didn't seem to be any rancour there. "And what line are you in then, Jake?"

Jake blinked. So, that was it? No digging into what had gone wrong?

Georgie watched her father warily. She really hadn't wanted to come to this party, the one bonus had been bringing the ultra-sexy Jake with her, which was bound to piss off the match-making Alfie and Carol, who wanted her to pair up with the respectable son of one of their respectable friends. Trouble was, Jake didn't look quite the same bad boy when he dressed up, he still looked sexy and edgy enough to make every woman in the room ogle, but he almost looked like the kind of respectable she'd been avoiding. Which was a bit shitty, so was the way Alfie and Carol were fawning over him.

But that wasn't the worst of it. She'd felt ill when she'd got up, and still felt decidedly rocky now, even worse now she'd worked out what was causing it. It was a bit like the morning after the night before, except she'd stayed in and ate chocolates while she watched a film. It was the kind of feeling that you were just waiting to come back. And dressing up to go out hadn't helped one bit. In fact, dressing up had made it worse.

Carol was almost pawing at Jake and a different kind of nausea bit at her. "I'll introduce Jake to a few *other* people shall I?" She linked her arm through his, any second now Carol would be asking if his intentions were honourable if she didn't do something, and quick.

"Oh, don't worry Georgina, I'm sure your father would love to have a man to man, you and I can have a catch up." The wicked witch had caught hold of his other arm, steering him the way she wanted. "We've not seen each other for ages." She gave a false cheery smile that made her flinch.

"It's been a few weeks, that's all." And I really don't want to talk to either of you.

Jake winked at her, untangled himself and squeezed her bum. Which was good and bad. Good for the naughty tingle, bad for the fact she'd been cornered. Shit, talking to Carol was not on the agenda at all. Talking to her father could be awkward, but Carol dug, deep. Like a bloody hormonal terrier that had lost a rat. At least Alfie kept it to the basics. Ten minutes in the Carol corner and she'd be owning up to shagging half the county, or bursting into tears and telling all. And she really didn't want to do either, but given the choice…

"We do miss you, you know."

Yeah, like a hole in the head. "I'm a bad influence on the children."

"We never said that."

Oh, God, the nice approach just made her feel guilty. Guilty for not being the perfect daughter, guilty for making their lives hell. "You didn't have to, it's pretty obvious even to me when I'm not welcome." Even as she said the words, her heart wasn't really in it. It was just habit, the easy way out.

"It's not that, we—"

"You."

Carol sighed. "It isn't that I don't want you here."

"Then why send me to boarding school? You didn't miss me then, did you?" Georgie slumped deeper into the chair, and half expected to be told to sit up straight. She was saying the things she'd always said, but somehow it didn't seem that important now. It was too long ago. And even if Carol had wanted her out of her hair back then, these days she offered enough olive branches to start up an oil bottling business. She wanted to be friends, and it was Carol, not anyone else who persistently texted to check she was okay. At one time she'd thought she was an interfering nosey old bat, but lately she hadn't been so sure. Lately it had been a comfort, knowing someone cared at least a tiny bit. Whatever her motives.

"We did miss you. I did. But we thought it was best for you. To have stability, something reliable. I mean we'd only just met, your father and I, and what if we'd split up and you'd been here? It would have been the same thing all over again. I would never have forgiven myself."

"Oh." She'd never thought of it that way.

"And we do want you back here now." Carol took a ladylike sip of her drink. "I don't think you're a bad influence on the children, but you're so much older than them, you want to do different things. I've always thought you must be completely bored out of your skull living with The Walton's."

Which was quite humorous for Carol. It deserved a bit of leeway. "Yeah, well, I guess you don't want them growing up like their big bad step-sister."

"I'd be very proud of them if they turned out like you have Georgina, but…"

Why do people always have to spoil it with a 'but'? She'd been doing so well.

"We, I, just sometimes worry that you're not happy, not very settled." She sat down on the chair next to Georgie, which was even more ominous. Sitting down meant they were there for the long haul.

"Maybe I don't want to be settled." We don't all see a mortgage, a man and a pile of nappies as worthy of a lifetime achievement award.

"Is this one serious?" She was watching Jake and Alfie across the room, deep in conversation, and Georgie cringed again, and put the half-drunk glass of champagne down on the floor. Partly to hide the fact that for some unidentifiable reason her hand was shaking, and partly because the bubbles were mixing very badly with the somersaulting of her stomach.

"We're just friends."

"Your father seems to like him."

Georgie shrugged. "He's nice enough."

"And you do like him, don't you? He's a good lad really, considering…"

"Considering what?" This evening was turning out a bit surreal. Carol trying to corner her and suffocate her into submission was fairly standard form, being nice about whoever was with her was weird, sounding almost like she understood was just plain spooky. And she still felt off, and even the half a glass of bubbly had been hard to swallow.

She stared at Carol. "Considering what?"

"Well, I just meant it must have been difficult with his father."

"His father?"

"In prison, and well his mother was never quite the same…." Her voice drifted and she looked awkward. Carol didn't like talking about 'unpleasant things'. "You did know?"

"Maybe." Maybe not.

"We would like to see you happy and settled dear." She brushed

Georgie's hair back over her shoulder, and she tried not to dodge away.

"I am happy."

"With someone who can look after you."

"I'm looking after myself fine, thanks."

"You like your new job?"

"I'm doing fine." She glanced up, her gaze clashing with Jake's.

"You look a bit tired, I just wondered about the late nights."

"There aren't many." And tonight was definitely not going to be one.

Carol was studying her, and uneasiness filtered through her body. It was a scrutiny, and for some reason she felt like wrapping her arms round her body and hiding. "You would tell us if there was something wrong? We are always here for you, you know."

"I'm sorry, I think I need to check Jake is all right, it's not fair to leave him." Georgie felt like her legs were going to give way beneath her as she clambered to her feet and headed for safety. Carol might be well meaning, but she was stifling, suffocating and Jake was a safe haven of neither. But she could still feel her step-mothers eyes on her as she reached the other side of the room, slipped her hand through his arm. "Do you mind if we go? I don't feel well."

"Your call, darling."

"Well, well if the bad penny hasn't turned up again. You always did like a bit of rough to entertain you, didn't you?" The upper class drawl swarmed over her like a nasty rash and Georgie felt her fingers tighten on Jake's arm.

"And you always did know how to sound a dick, Ashley."

She turned on the smile that was close to an automatic response when people like Ashley Grant came within spitting distance. All authority and no backbone.

"Ah, but I heard you liked dicks."

"Not your kind. Did you want something?"

He was staring at her tits as though any second now he was

going to bury his face in them, and the shiver of disdain ran straight down Georgie's spine and back up again.

"Yes." He smiled a dirty smile that did nothing for her at all. Well, it did make her feel slightly more bilious. "You, for old time's sakes."

"There are no old times, Ashley." She could have added 'and you never had me' but she didn't. Getting away was more of a priority than fielding his stupid comments.

"We were good together. Worth another try I'd say."

"You're either drunk or mixing me up with someone else." She'd had to put up with the groping Ashley on more than one occasion, during those years when she'd objected less to her family's misguided attempts to pair her off. On paper, Ashley was perfect. In the flesh he was a leering, pawing, bad imitation of his father. The first time his clammy hand had shot up her skirt was also the last time. But the arrogance of his upbringing had convinced him he'd been close to scoring. And now three sheets to the wind he'd decided the time had come.

"Come on, be honest, stop wasting time with losers like him and admit you want a bit more of the Grant glamour inside you, that slutty side of you is such a turn on." He'd moved closer, so that she felt like the filling in a sandwich. Backed up against a silent Jake, her exit blocked off by the halitosis bloom that preceded Ashley. Bad breath and expensive aftershave were not mingling well with the half a glass of champagne that was planning a revolt of its own from the depths of her churning stomach. His hand was aiming for her boob like some wobbly undecided Exocet missile.

"Keep your hands to yourself."

Ashley was too pissed to take in the warning, and it wasn't just his hands he had plans for. His mouth already on its way to hers, wide open, tongue flopping like a beached whale. She closed her eyes, wondering if she could get away with a knee in his engorged groin, when she realised he'd not got to his target. Jake had. Large tanned hands wrapped around the lapels of the other man's jacket in a gesture that looked casual, but she just knew wasn't. "The lady said let go." His voice was mild, like he was talking to a backwards child. Which wasn't far off the mark.

Ashley stared back, weighing up his opponent. "Lady? You must be fucking—"

"Yes, I am actually. And you're not. Now you can walk away or I'm quite happy to discuss it… somewhere quieter." He brushed a finger slowly down the man's lapel, flicked away an imaginary speck of dust. And it was as though Georgie could actually see Ashley's lust turn tail and run.

"I'd heard you were back with your old faggot of a painter actually." *Better than a city wanker.* She muttered it under her breath, but from the look Jake sent her she had a horrible feeling he'd heard. "Still modelling for him, are you? I bet your pa isn't too happy that you've gone into a partnership with him, is he? From what I heard—"

What he'd heard, Georgie never found out because Jake's fingers had tightened on his jacket in a way he didn't seem comfortable with at all. He dried up, the thin ungenerous lips pressed firmly together. And Georgie found herself being none too gently steered towards the door.

***

The air outside was cold, icy fingers that shot straight to her lungs and made her draw a sharp breath, but it still felt better than being inside.

"Friend of yours?"

"A family acquaintance." She tried to stop the shivering that seemed to have invaded her body. "The type they'd love to see me hitched to."

"Ah, yes, the old time's sake."

"We never—"

"It's none of my business."

"But."

He draped his jacket around her shoulders, stopped her protestation dead. He didn't want to know. He'd rescued her, like he had before. But, he probably believed every word. Or he didn't care.

"You okay?"

"Yes, I am now." She forced the jitters down, along with the brief pang of reality. He'd saved her again, but just because it was what he did. He would have done it for anyone. "Thanks."

"You're welcome."

"Jake?" Her heels crunched on the driveway, the sound of clinking glasses and laughter echoing behind them.

He opened the car door for her, slammed it shut and made his way round to the passenger side. Settled himself into her small car, put the seatbelt on before he half turned to look at her. "That sounds ominous."

"It's not." She turned the key in the ignition, waited for the windscreen to start to clear. She hadn't realised until now that she knew practically nothing about him. He'd been the bad boy at school, the one who wagged off, who smoked behind the bike sheds. She hadn't even realised he liked horses. All she'd done was have wild sex with him and drag him to that awful party. And threaten to pull the rug from under his feet, his land. Even Carol and Alfie seemed to know more about him than she did. "It's just Carol said..." She was everything he'd accused her of. Shallow, spoiled, ungrateful.

He folded his arms and his face hardened, just that tiny bit that made him look forbidding rather than easy going.

"She said your father was in prison."

"And?"

"It's true then?"

He sighed, shook his head slightly, and then turned to stare out of the windscreen. "Let's drive shall we? Then maybe we can talk later."

He didn't say another single word on the drive back, and it should have felt awkward, but it didn't. Georgie concentrated on the road and all she could think of was the few words Carol had said. They spun round in her head, growing multiplying until the uneasy feeling started to harden into a conviction that things were going very wrong.

She pulled up in front of the apartment and he got out wordlessly. Followed her in, sat down, elbows on his knees, chin on his knuckles before finally giving her the long stare.

"He burned our home down, well he switched on the gas and threw a match to be more precise. Boom. Asshole." The first words he'd said since they'd set off back cut through the silence. "He turned out to be a complete loser who just took the easy route out."

"Oh." Wasn't expecting that. "Erm, why did he need a way out?"

He stared straight through her. "Money. Isn't that the root of all evil?" For a brief moment he focussed on her, his mouth curled into something that wasn't humour. "He was a gambler who thought he could play the system, thought that if he bet long and hard enough he could climb out of the hole he was in. He lost his job and because of who he was he couldn't get another one, so every penny Mum earned he took to the pub or the betting shop. And she let him, the idiot."

"Maybe she loved him?"

"Oh yeah, she loved him. What was it you said, just another four letter word?" The short croak of a laugh cut into her. "Too fucking right. Once he was in the slammer that was it, I hardly saw her. Spent all her time visiting him or thinking about visiting him." He put his feet up on the table, settled back, one arm across his body, and then reached out with his other, pulled her close so she couldn't look at him.

"But he's out now? You've seen him?" She rested her head against the broad familiar shoulder. Drank in the unfamiliar smell of his aftershave.

"I don't know, and I don't give a fuck." His fingers briefly curled into her shoulder. "I don't want to be with a loser like that."

Which explained why Rowena wanted him to commit, to do something. But she hadn't thought his dad was a loser, she'd said he was good. And so had Georgie's dad.

"I was doing my own thing, scraping by, then I got talking to Rowena at a horse auction. There was this horse going for meat money because it was wild and I'd offered the guy fifty quid just to stop him bloody trotting the poor lame thing up and down, it was scared shitless and I could just see it taking off or breaking down. He hadn't even entered it in the sale, was just out to make a quick buck. She saw him hand the lead rope over and she must have seen the look on my face. She offered to pay for a trailer to shift it and told me I could keep it at her place, said she trusted me to do the right thing by it."

"Why? Because it's in your blood?"

He paused, the wait lengthened. She'd thrown his words back at him. All she could think of was those words from Carol, the comments she'd half missed, his throwaway 'in my blood'. Just who the hell was he? She wanted to know, she needed to know. Before she told him.

She'd stepped back into her past and expected it to be like it was then, simple. Him the bad boy, her the good girl.

Except she wasn't quite sure how it worked now, now that she wasn't the innocent she used to be, and Jake, well in Jake she'd seen a glimpse of something that was as reliable and moral as it could get. Confused just didn't cover it.

"It's the blood I don't want, but you can't choose can you? My dad was a pikey, a gypsy, who married a settler. So lose-lose eh? Her family hated him, his lot hated her. And he tried to settle, buy a place but cocked it up. Not easy to make it where you're not wanted."

"But he tried."

He ignored her. "There was always a horse around, he couldn't not have one, it was the one thing he knew how to do, so he groomed and when I wasn't fixing bikes I was fixing horses. Not like you mind you, no hoity toity horse shows, we were for sorting and selling."

"How do you know my dad so well then?"

"He bought that black mare of yours from my dad, I rode to show him what she could do."

"He bought Salsa from you?" She could hear the trace of disbelief in her own voice. He half grinned, that cocky look that grabbed her somewhere inside.

"Salsa? What kind of a name is that?"

She decided to ignore that. "So I can blame all those bloody bruises on you, you bugger."

"I used to come and watch you ride." His fingers stroked down her arm, gentle, mesmerising, circles that touched something deep under her skin. "Hide under the hedge."

"Why?"

"Wanted to see what you were made of." He stopped abruptly, pulled back, sat up straighter. "I better go."

"Stay."

"I thought you felt ill?"

"Not that ill."

He grinned. "I'm not bringing the motorbike in if that's what's on your mind."

"We can manage without." She traced her finger slowly down the front of his shirt. His hand covered hers, stopped her progress.

"Why were you in such a hurry to get out of there?"

"Oh, she started talking the whole happy ever after crap, bawling babies included. Love and romance isn't my bag."

"You might want that one day." He was looking at her lazily now.

"No." It came out too sharp. "I've never wanted kids."

"Sounds a bit final."

"It is." Or it had been. Bugger.

"No maternal instinct in there then." He raised an eyebrow, put a large, capable hand over her heart.

Nope, she hadn't thought a single maternal instinct existed in her at all. Babies were bad news. If it hadn't been for her mum getting pregnant she might never have left them, well there was no might about it. She wouldn't. And if Carol and Alfie hadn't got so cosy and started breeding then she wouldn't have been uprooted and sent away to that god-awful school. Which left her with a major problem she was trying to ignore for the time being.

She fought for a light tone because the look he was giving her was far too intense. "Nope. Give me a puppy any day." A wave of something that had to be tiredness flooded her body, it was all too hard, all too complicated. "Why? Do you want to go forth and multiply?"

"Spread my wonderful genes?" He laughed, his hand drifting down to her breast. "Nope, but I'd quite like to get some practice in."

Oh God, right now she wanted him, needed him, but it wasn't right. It was all going wrong. She'd had stupid daydreams about going back, and she couldn't. She had no right to cock up his life, when it wouldn't make any difference to hers anyway. Which appeared to be well and truly fucked up right now.

"Will you just hold me?"

He did. Wrapping his arms round her, pulling her in tight. And it felt good, too good to spoil. "Are you okay?" His words were muffled against her hair and she didn't quite know what to say, whether she was all right or all wrong. She just wanted to stay here though. Held. For the first time in years she felt safe, but she also felt scared stiff.

"I'm fine." Why couldn't she just stop right there? Leave it at that, all cosy and nice? "Jake, have you ever thought about settling down, is it just me that's strange?" Okay Georgie, shoot that safe feeling to shreds.

"Settle?" He laughed, rich and deep, his body reverberating

against hers. "You and me might be as different as night and day darling, but the one thing we've got in common is we're never going to say 'I do.'"

She felt sick, a real deep down desperation. She had to tell him, explain what was really bothering her, the real reason for running out of the party, but she couldn't. Telling him would complicate everything even more than the stupid patch of grass was doing. Even if at the back of her mind there'd been that slight wavering doubt, that feeling maybe she could stop one day. Be with one person. Be happy. But that man wasn't Jake. And it wasn't a real feeling, it was stupid hormones.

"Maybe it's the gypsy blood, the need to keep moving. What's your excuse?" His hand was warm against her leg.

"I'm just better on my own." She covered it with her own, suddenly feeling too drained to do anything. Suddenly needing to be on her own, the lust slipping right off the radar. "You're right. I am tired. Maybe we should call it a day."

"Sure." He was up before she could say another word. "I'll let myself out, you get some sleep."

This wasn't how the evening should end. She wanted to call him back, tell him she was scared, tell him she had a decision to make but she didn't even know where to start. She had to bloody tell him.

"Thanks for coming with me tonight."

He raised a hand. "It was an interesting experience."

"Not the word I normally use."

"Carol wasn't quite what I expected." It was the non-judgemental tone that did it. Gave her an out.

"I don't think she's had an easy time with me, has she?"

"Has anyone?" He laughed.

Maybe Carol just wanted everything for her that she'd always craved for herself. Stable home, everyone being nice to each other, steady type of job that's suitable for a girl, and a nice husband to provide. But Georgie had wanted something far different. And been far too stubborn to meet her half way, to try and understand.

"You were upset and hurting, Georgie." He ruffled her hair. "Kids and parents sometimes live on different planets."

Yeah, but I'm not a kid any longer. She could see that now. "We're totally different people."

"You are, and it doesn't make either of you bad. Night, Georgina."

He took a step towards the door, and she wanted to shout come back, but she couldn't. What would she say anyway? Stay, I need you, let's talk babies.

"Jake. I want to—"

"You don't need to explain anything. You're right, let's call it a day."

"I didn't mean..." *I don't want to call it a day. I want you to stay. I need to tell you something.*

Chapter Nine

"You sure you're up to this?" Jake was holding the reins of a horse and giving her a strange look.

"I'm fine. Come on, let's get on with it."

"You look shit."

"Thanks for that, it's made me feel much better." She'd spent all night awake, trying not to think about Jake, trying to work out how to sort out the mess she'd created. He'd lost more than she had, back then when they were on the cusp of growing up. She'd lost her mum, but her dad had still been there. She could see that, even if he'd turned into a man she hardly knew. But he was there, she had someone. And she'd had Carol, except she'd done her damnedest to chase her away, to blame her for everything.

Jake had been left with nothing, and Rowena had been the one who'd believed in him. Given him a chance. Let him do what he was good at.

Until she'd walked in like some spoiled kid and demanded the toys.

She knew she looked crap, she hadn't even needed a mirror to tell her that. Let alone Jake.

But she couldn't tell him about the baby. Not yet. She would do, once she'd worked out how to stop the feeling that she was going to burst into tears. That just had to be the hormones. She didn't do tears, at least not because of the look on a man's face. She'd felt closer to him last night than she had with anyone in a long time, even though she hardly knew him. For a brief moment it had been kittens and rainbows, a scary scene of domesticity. Then real life had stuck its oar in. They were totally different. No way did he ever want to settle. This was all about lust and a tenuous shared past.

She could do something for him though. And she would. She'd knock her crazy dream on the head, tell him calmly what the problem was, then come up with a plan B, or C, or whatever she'd now got up to. Yeah, she'd explain. Sure she would. Soon.

"Earth to Georgie."

"Sorry, just felt a bit dizzy."

"We're not doing this."

"Don't be stupid."

"One buck and you'll be in the dirt. Look," he had his hands on her shoulders, steady eyes gazing straight to her soul. And just like that, she knew. She'd got it worse than she'd imagined. It wasn't just the shock of the whole pregnancy thing, she'd been falling for him. Falling for a man who was totally allergic to anything that looked like stability, a man who thought she was a spoiled brat. "You don't have to prove anything here."

Oh yeah, sure.

"You look rough so we'll do it tomorrow."

"I'm fine. Can we just get on with it, please?"

"And have you puke all over the saddle I just cleaned?"

"Ah, it's the saddle you're bothered about, not me."

"Too true." But he was still staring at her. She glanced down.

"I didn't sleep with him, you know."

"Whoa, where did that come from?"

She shrugged. "I just wanted you to know, and the thing with Sly was a five minute wonder, for what it's worth." She was babbling, but she just wanted him to see something good in her. Realise, before it ended, that she wasn't what he thought.

"Georgina." His hand was on her chin and she wanted to brush against it like a fawning cat, feel his warmth. Instead she froze. Safer. Less chance of looking an idiot. "That guy was right last night, you deserve someone a lot better than me." The words were soft, but every one hit her like a splinter of shrapnel. "I'm a bit of rough for you, and you're too posh for me."

"At least you didn't say posh totty."

"I didn't."

"You're not—"

"My dad made one big mistake, trying to be someone he wasn't. And I'm not going to do the same." Which pretty much made that clear. And he was right. So right. She just fancied him, she didn't want him. "I'm not a loser, but I'm not a lot of other things either."

"Are you going to give me a leg up on this horse or not?"

"Not."

"Fine. I'll go then if I'm not wanted."

"Sure." He had already stepped away, was walking off, leading the horse with him. Which put her firmly in her place. He paused, turned and studied her, moss green eyes soft with something she couldn't quite fathom out. "Come back in a couple of hours if you feel up to it."

God, she felt like a begging dog being thrown crumbs. Disappointment had been clawing at her stomach one second, followed by a surge of relief the next. Or maybe that was just the early morning coffee that no longer seemed to agree with her.

"Jake?" He paused, but didn't turn to look at her. "Did you talk to Rowena, you know about…?"

"I did." His voice was soft, steady.

So, he'd made his bid, just like she had. Was waiting for judgement day. Just like she'd been. Until she'd found out about the baby. And suddenly life had shifted on its axis, turned right into wrong, important into trivial. "You really care about this place don't you?"

"I care about Rowena, she was there for me. She's the only person who's been there for me." The horse rubbed her head along his shoulder, but he didn't flinch.

"Do you hate me for barging into your life?"

He did look at her then. "I don't hate you, Georgina." The soft voice crept along her body, under her skin, tugged at something inside her and she felt like crying. Kicking and screaming like some kid that it wasn't fair.

"I really missed this place, you know."

"Did you miss the place, or the way things were?"

She rolled the lining of her jeans pocket between thumb and forefinger. "I miss," she missed her dad, her horse, she missed all the perfect little things that had made up her life. "I miss the life I might have had."

"You can make a different one, Georgie. We're all here to make our own lives."

"That's what I was trying to do." Hot tears burned her eyes, threatened to spill. She bit down in her bottom lip, waited for the feelings to go.

"And you don't have to lie to me about that man. He's your business."

"I haven't lied to you."

"Don't take me for a fool, Georgie. Call it a partnership, business, whatever you like, but don't try and pull the wool over my eyes."

"I'm not, honestly."

"Look, you promised not to bring him here again and I turn my back for one minute and the pair of you are sneaking about."

"I—"

"The day of the party? I mean, how can you think, in this place I wouldn't find out?"

"He needed to check a few things, and I thought—"

"Let's face it, you didn't think."

"I'm sorry, honestly. He wasn't here for long."

"Long enough for your mates at the party to know about it."

"Is that what you're bothered about?"

"I'm bothered about you, Georgie. Not them. And all the furtive calls and texts, do you think I'm stupid?"

"I didn't want to upset you." And she hadn't. But she'd needed to talk to Sly, to sort things out. He'd been enthusiastic, and without him she couldn't make it work. Except now maybe it didn't matter. "I'm sorry, Jake. I wasn't being sneaky, but I know you don't like him and it just seemed easier…"

His unsmiling face studied her, and she hadn't got a clue what was going through his head. Then he clicked at the horse, stepped away. She stared at his back as he headed for the stables, then as soon as she was sure he was out of sight she clambered over the fence and headed over towards Rowena's cottage.

***

"I don't want you to tell me why." Rowena handed her a mug of what looked like dirty dish water but smelled of a garden in summertime and settled herself into the armchair opposite. Maybe it was a mistake to come here. She took a sip of the hot liquid and felt relief as it headed straight down her throat with no sign of a u-turn. "But just be sure you know the real reason before you talk to him."

"I do, I—"

She held a hand up, then indicated the cup. "Drink up, it'll make you feel better."

Georgie cringed inwardly at the assessing look that was directed her way. "I feel—"

"Fine? Yes, I'm sure you do. Now, dear," Rowena retreated further into the old armchair which seemed to be engulfing her like an old hairy blanket. "Tell me about your father and the party."

Georgie stared, she could have sworn the older woman's eyes were shining with what looked like devilment. Nope, she had to be losing it. Seriously. Maybe there was more than herbal tea in this cup. She looked down at it suspiciously.

"What did he have to say about you taking Jake?"

"Jake?"

"You did take him along to the party, didn't you?"

"I didn't want to go on my own."

Rowena chuckled. "I'd be more than happy to have Jake with me if I was twenty years younger."

Forty more like, she bit back the retort and wondered where this was going.

"He always was a bit of a character, even as a child, had his father's sense of adventure and his mother's gentle touch. They were such a lovely couple, devoted, so sad. Ah well, I suppose you'll want to get off then?"

Georgie stared. No, getting off hadn't been at the forefront of her mind, but it seemed it had just been promoted to pole position. She'd been hoping her idea would be welcomed with open arms, that her generous gesture would be appreciated for what it was. Instead she felt like she was being given the brush off.

"I can't tell you what to do child." It was like she'd read her mind. Georgie put the cup down with an abrupt clatter and stood up. "But sometimes the obvious way out isn't the right way."

"I thought you'd be pleased, it's what you want isn't it?"

"This isn't about me, Georgina. I'm sure you mean well, but try seeing it from the other side of the fence."

"Well it's what he wants."

"Do you know that? Have you asked him?"

Just what she needed, wacky tea and cryptic comments. Here she was, about to make a sacrifice and she was being preached at, and she couldn't understand a bloody word of it.

"You imagine how you'd feel if the boot was on the other foot. Don't rush it dear, that's all I'm saying. Oh, now look at the time, aren't you supposed to be helping Jake with that horse of his before it goes dark?"

"Have you been watching us?" That was all she needed right now.

Rowena grinned. "I keep an eye on the place."

Brilliant. Now she had to work out a list of places not to jump him. Not that she'd ever get the chance to do it again the way things were going.

"You look after yourself dear, give Jake my love and tell him I'll see him tomorrow."

Look after herself, what kind of a thing was that to say? Her hand went instinctively to her stomach and out of the corner of her eye she saw a look that could have been smug satisfaction on the older woman's face. Great. Everyone knew. Apart from Jake.

She went back the long way round. All the way down the long driveway until it met the lane, a few steps to the right, then through the next gateway and all the way up a very similar driveway until she was back at Jake's barn. He wasn't with the mare. She tracked him down, which wasn't hard all she had to do was follow the whistle, to an empty loosebox where he was fiddling with his motorbike.

"Are we working the mare?"

"Not today." He glanced up, half smiled, the curls on his forehead damp with perspiration. Curls she wanted to reach out and touch. He was in his leathers, dark and deadly. While she'd been sipping hallucinogenic tea he'd obviously taken the bike out.

"You've been out."

"I needed to think."

"Oh?"

"So." He stopped fiddling and looked at her. "What did you want to talk about?"

"Who said I came here to talk?"

"You're twitching like a horse at the starting gate. Better out than in as they say."

Oh, if only he knew. She tipped a bucket over, perched on the edge of it.

"I've been thinking too. It's just, I thought." She crossed her arms, stared at the dirt floor and took a deep breath. And she told him. Just like that. About the new plan, Plan B, before she had a chance to think it over, change her mind.

Silence. Nothing. Not even the sound of his breathing or the cough of a horse. So she had to look up.

Jake stared at her, then stared some more. And she could see the chasm between them open up, a gulf so deep that no would dare try and jump over. "No."

"Don't just say no like that, think about it, listen to me."

"I don't want to listen, Georgina. I'm done with listening."

"But I want you to have it." She'd been thinking about it all night, about what she was going to do to sort the whole mess. And there was only one answer. She'd buy the land, and give it to Jake. For a brief nanosecond she'd thought maybe they could do this together, then she'd realised she was being stupid. There was no together. He'd made that more than clear this morning. Which had only left one option.

"No, I'm sorry, you can't buy me like that."

"I'm not trying to buy you."

"I don't want charity, and I'm not taking this from you."

Georgie stared and every answer she'd had prepared in her head shot out. It had been bad when her mother had walked out on her, hurt when she'd realised she had no place in Alfie and Carol's life. And now he was kicking her in the teeth. This land had been the one thing she had that she could give him. Her sacrifice, and he was throwing it straight back in her face. "It's not like that."

"Well, what is it like then? What are you, Lady Bountiful bestowing gifts? You've done a deal with Rowena, then fine. Keep the fucking land and let me run my life my own way."

"I haven't done a deal, it wasn't like that. I wouldn't do that to you. But you can't afford it, and I can."

He stood up abruptly, took a step close, over that chasm. He squatted down and she flinched, but when he raised his hands to her face his touch was so gentle it sent a shiver over her skin. Those deep forest eyes were staring straight into hers. "You can't keep me here that way, Georgie. I'll only stay if I want to."

"I'm not trying to keep you here. I'm going, leaving. If it was about tying you down I'd—" The words froze on her tongue.

"What? Seduce me?" The tip of his mouth was curled in the cruel semblance of the smile she so wanted to see before she went. "Before you bugger off?"

"I'd tell you I was pregnant."

Chapter Ten

Now she did feel sick. Really sick and it was nothing to do with the unbalanced hormones which had been sending her haywire the last few days. She hadn't meant to say that at all. That was later. When everything was sorted. Just before she left.

"You're pregnant?" He was on his feet, the angry clatter of his feet against a bucket. His voice so low and incredulous that she could have imagined the gentle tone it had replaced.

She nodded.

"And you're leaving?"

Now was the time to say she didn't want to go, but she couldn't. The words just wouldn't come.

"I thought it was best." Because you don't want me, you don't want a baby. Together we'd be a disaster.

"So that's what this is all about." His voice was dangerously low now, too soft. "You really are going into partnership aren't you? Pretty good going for a girl who swore to me the other day that she hated babies and didn't want to settle down." He shoved his hands deep into his pockets, gave a sharp bark of a laugh and glared. "And you thought you'd give me a nice little leaving present." Scathing was not the word for it. "So the whole artist retreat thing, helping with the business plan, was that just an excuse to see each other? Or, no—"

"Jake stop. Just stop it. It's not like that."

"Stop? Why?"

"You're being stupid, just listen."

"Oh, I'm done with listening. I know, I bet the pair of you were planning on taking over the village, weren't you? Then you got pregnant and decided to drop the idea. So, the parties over eh? You've had your fun and you're waltzing off somewhere better. What I don't get is where I fit in."

"Jake, you don't fit in." She meant there wasn't anything to 'fit in' to. No plan, nothing, but he wasn't listening.

"No, I don't, do I? Oh I remember, I'm just the bit of rough. Well, you bugger off with your artist and enjoy the rest of your life then, but skip the leaving presents, eh? If I want to stay then I'll work it out myself thank you."

Shit, he thought she was back with Sly. He really believed that what he'd seen in the barn was real. Now was the time to say that there was no 'her and anyone else'. But something stopped her. Something like the shrivelling look he was giving her. The look that said we're as different as night and day, and I despise you. Getting pregnant was bad, falling for him was worse.

"It never really did mean anything to you this place did it? For a moment back there I thought it did, but it's all just a game isn't it? Including me."

"Being with you was never a game."

"Oh, I was just handy on the side lines? Someone to fill in the boring bits while you were waiting to hatch your plan."

"It wasn't like that, it isn't like that."

"Well you just tell me how it was then before you go. Or aren't I worth the explanation?"

"There wasn't a plan, you have to believe me Jake."

"So why are you going?"

"I..." What could she say? I'm going because I don't want to wreck both our lives? I'm going because if I don't it will be like Mum and Dad all over again. I'm going before I make you hate me?

"Fine. Have it your way then, you buy the fucking land and keep it for yourself, breed babies on it, seeing as it looks like you've already got it all done and dusted. But don't come back here until you're giving me my marching orders, okay?" He'd backed away as he spoke, was next to his motorbike, pushing it effortlessly off its stand. Was wheeling it past her as she floundered for words. "Shut the gate when you go."

"That's it, just sod off, run away."

He got on the bike. Turned the key.

"Run away, isn't that what you always do instead of listening to what anyone is trying to tell you? I didn't mean to get friggin' pregnant." Revved up the engine to drown her out. "Jake, Jake wait, please. I want to buy it for you. I haven't seen Sly since…" But she was talking to thin air.

***

Georgie jumped at the sound of metal against wood. The mare who'd been disturbed by the noise, or just hungry for more hay was kicking out at her door. Breaking the heavy silence that had replaced the angry roar of the motorbike.

For a moment she hesitated. It wasn't her horse, she had no right to be here. Then she wandered over to the stall, let herself in, rested a hand on the dappled grey neck. "I wanted to buy it for him." She moved in closer, wrapped one hand under the muscled neck, stroked her other along it, leaning in, taking in the smell of warm horse and hay. "Because I love him." God, she was stupid, so bloody stupid. She closed her eyes, to keep the threatening tears where they belonged.

The horse rubbed velvet soft lips against the back of her neck, enjoying the closeness. "I wanted to give him the one thing that really meant something to me, not because it was easy, not to buy him off." Oh, God, she mustn't cry. The rhythmic motion of her hand seemed to flow through her body, releasing all the useless

124

words she should have said before. "Why didn't I listen to Rowena?" The horse nibbled at her hair. "Why am I so fucking stupid?"

"Because you care?"

Georgie jumped like she'd been stung by a hornet, and spun round so fast that the mare threw her head up then back down, its hard jaw crashing into her head. "Shit." She rubbed at the tender spot which seemed to have mushroomed out from somewhere on the crown of her head all the way to her teeth. "What are you doing here?"

He smiled, took the last remaining step to the stall door, holding out a hand to the mare who recognised an apology when she saw one and stepped forward to see if there was food on offer. "Would you rather I wasn't?" His tone was even, but she could sense the tension, the wait for a rejection he was half expecting.

"No" She shrugged, felt like a kid caught out behind the bike shed. "It's just I wasn't expecting you. Are you looking for Jake? He's not here right now."

"I'm looking for you actually. Not changed much, has it?" He was gazing round, taking in every cobweb that the weak sunlight had picked out. "We had some good times here, didn't we?"

For once there wasn't a note of judgement. None of the guarded tone that she'd come to expect from Alfie, this was more like Dad, the man she'd almost forgotten. She closed her eyes, opened them again and it wasn't a dream. She hadn't been whisked back to some perfectly preserved past. Just her father and herself in a dusty cobweb strewn barn.

"Yes." She tried it again, louder this time. "Yes, we did."

"It used to scare me stiff sometimes, watching you ride that mad horse. I used to have nightmares about what your mother would do to us if anything had happened to you. She hated us coming here you know." His gaze was flicking between her and the horse, then he straightened up. "I got home from work one day and she'd advertised the horse, had a string of people interested."

"She what?" Georgie forgot about keeping her distance.

"She would have preferred it if you'd taken up ballet."

"She tried to sell Salsa? Really?"

"Just being a protective mother." He stroked his finger along the door of the stall. "Horses were just big things with teeth at one end and kicking hooves at the other, and we did leave her out a bit."

"Oh, but…"

"I think that's partly why she found," he paused, "other interests. She was lonely and I was too busy to notice."

"So, it was—"

"It was my fault, not yours, honey. I was being selfish, keeping you to myself too much. And, at the end of the day your mother and I were two very different people."

Just like Jake and me. "How did you know I was here?"

"Jake told me, at the party, all about how you two had met. He's an interesting guy." He looked at her pointedly, so she glared back. He laughed. "Okay, it's none of my business. But I did like him, not your usual yes man."

Nope. "We're not involved."

"I didn't come here to quiz you about your personal life." *So why did you come?* "Carol was worried about you, she does care, you know."

"I know." She did deep down. She'd done a lot of thinking since the party, about the past. About being the step-daughter from hell. Maybe she'd been the problem, not Carol. Okay, they'd clashed. But what mother and daughter didn't? She couldn't even begin to imagine how she'd deal with a daughter of her own that was difficult, but dealing with one that had just been abandoned by her own mother? An involuntary shiver found its way down her spine.

"Are you okay?"

"I'm fine. So you came because Carol wanted you to?"

He laughed. "Not just because of that, I have always done what I think is right for you, you know." She shrugged. "To be honest I wanted an excuse to come back and see the old place." He put his hands in his pockets. "Shame we can't turn the clock back, eh?"

She couldn't remember the last time she'd looked into his eyes, properly. They'd not had the time, or the inclination, for too many years to count. But she was looking now, and he was looking straight back. "We can't though, can we?"

"We can't, no, but maybe we can back track a bit?"

"I think I've been trying to do that." She opened the door, stepped out of the stall and locked it firmly. Slowly.

"Dad?"

"Yep."

"Why did you sell up?" Sell out.

He wandered over to the patch of light that burst through the large open doorway, the one patch of brightness in the gloom of the barn. Stared out at the fields beyond. "This place was all the best bits of your childhood and all the worst bits of my marriage. It was success, the embodiment of our relationship and it was total failure. I didn't want a reminder." He spun on his heel and looked back at her. "It's the hurt that you want to sweep away, and sometimes when you do it you don't realise what else is getting dumped at the same time." He shrugged, a gesture she recognised as her own. "At the time I just thought we hadn't got any horse and there was no reason you'd want to hang on to it. I'm sorry George." Nobody called her George, but Dad. Georgie, yes, and Georgina, but George was what he used to call her. Or his little Georgie Porgy, as he tossed her in the air, or legged her up into the saddle. Before the horses she'd been George and he'd been the dragon.

"Does it make you happy or sad being back here?"

The question caught her by surprise. She wasn't sure any more. At first she'd been nervous, then it had been a trip down memory lane, nostalgia station first stop. Then she'd been happy, but she could see now that the happiness was more to do with Jake than just the place.

"Is that offer of a job still open? I mean just as a temporary thing, if I wanted it. But I'm not sure yet."

"It is. You know I'd love to have you working for us, you did a solid job when you filled in over your summer break."

"It would just be temporary. I don't want anything permanent."

"And?"

"I can't live with you, I mean I don't want to, I want my own place."

"We could sort a short term contract, if you're sure that's what you want."

"I don't know yet. And I want a proper contract, and no favouritism. And I don't want you to interfere in my personal life." She dared to look up, he was smiling, holding his hands up. "Or tell me which men I should be dating."

He smiled, the slow, gentle, caring smile that she used to see so often. "Is that what you really want, Georgie? What about this place?" He paused and the question he didn't ask hung in the air, what about Jake?

What did she want? That was the, as in capital THE big question. What she wanted and what she'd decided she had to settle for were two very different things.

She walked over to her father, slipped her hand through his arm and stared out at the trees, the paddocks studded with hoof marks. Whatever she'd been planning originally, it had all changed now. She could see that it was history repeating itself. Her having a baby, it coming here at weekends to see its father, play with the horses. While she waited. Somewhere else. Jealous of a child who saw more of the man she loved than she did. What would happen next, would she be a runaway mother like her mum had been? She couldn't, she just couldn't watch the same scene replay here. That wasn't what was supposed to happen. She could break down and wail like a child, or she could be the independent woman that Jake actually seemed a tiny bit fond of. Or he had been.

"Can I treat you to a coffee?" Alfie had covered her cold hand with his, snapped her out of her thoughts. "In town?"

"Sounds good to me."

"Don't rush it, George. Don't make the same mistake I did."

Oh boy, if he knew the mistake she'd made he really wouldn't be quite as calm, and she sure as hell wasn't going to spoil the moment and tell him.

"I just want to leave a note, then I'm ready to go."

***

Jake was shaking. Tremors rolling down his arms as he revved the bike up and turned onto the lane. This time it was nothing to do with the engine, it was anger, pure anger cascading from him until it hurt.

He'd not realised just how much of his heart was in this place until she'd blithely told him what she'd done. Until she'd told him she'd broken every rule, cut through their agreement. Set her own rules, like she'd always done. He'd just been a minor obstacle in the way. The road blurred ahead and he pushed the helmet visor up angrily, but the mist didn't shift. He pulled in, his heart hammering and all he could think was that the girl he'd fallen for had taken him for a fool. Drawn him in and spat him out.

Yeah, fallen for. It had gradually dawned on him that he missed her when she wasn't there, he worried about her when she'd looked pale and drawn. Because she was pregnant. With the child of that long haired pretentious old artist she'd been seeing between shags with him. He'd assumed that when she brought that man here it had been a one off, more fool him. He'd obviously been part of the plan from the start, taking the opportunity to have a quick one, in his frigging barn. Helping with the business plan my arse.

She'd come waltzing in with her eye on the prize, and he'd fallen for every line she'd thrown his way. Let her under his defences and into the place while all the time old Sly was in the background waiting to stake his claim. Yeah, once she'd found out she was pregnant she'd lost interest in reliving her childhood dreams.

How could she walk in so calmly and tell him that she was

129

going? That it was over and the land was a leaving present, and in the next breath tell him she was pregnant. Ready to start afresh. With someone else. He'd been an idiot to dismiss that lingering moment between her and her artist, a fool to try and ignore the fact that it was common knowledge in the village that she was going into partnership with him. Knowledge that no-one had thought to share with him. Not that he'd have listened.

He'd fallen for every line about how she didn't want to settle, didn't want a family, been blind to the bleeding obvious.

Jake took his helmet off, wiped his forearm across his eyes. The mist cleared, but the lump in his throat didn't. Somehow it didn't add up. She'd loosened up when they'd been working the horses, looked like she was genuinely having fun. That laugh wasn't fake. It couldn't have been.

And at the party she'd been at his side when she didn't need to be, laughing, joking but catching his eye whenever he looked her way. Okay, her parents hated Sly, so she couldn't take him. But if they were planning on setting up, having a baby, why pretend?

Spoilt she might be, but she wasn't really a wild child, the bad girl she pretended to be. Maybe it was really one last generous gesture before she went. Maybe she had been trying to be nice. She didn't owe him anything. She was off to get married, forget her little scheme. Move on with her life. And this patch of land suddenly wasn't as important to her. She was handing it over. Leaving him how she'd found him. But with cash in Rowena's pocket and the place he wanted in his. Free. Gratis.

Except it wouldn't be the same. She'd be gone. And owning this land would tie him to it, take away his freedom for ever. Shackle him, just like his father had been. And a rich girl called Georgie would be responsible. If he could hack it, he'd always feel he owed her, and he didn't want to owe anyone. If his dad hadn't had debts then life would never had got nasty. And if he couldn't hack it, if it all went wrong he'd hate her for doing it to him.

Jake stared up at the sky. Did his father hate his mother? He doubted it. They were stuck together like superglue. When they'd committed it had been total, forever. She forgave him his sins, his wandering eye and wandering spirit. And he forgave her for changing his life, trapping him. But maybe he'd never felt trapped.

He closed his eyes. Took a deep breath. He didn't want to hate Georgina. He'd grown to like her more than he ever thought he could. Admired her for the way she got stuck in, recognised that she wasn't being spoiled or grabbing. Misguided maybe. Stupid to hook up with a washed out has been who was old enough to be her father. But hey, who was he to judge?

He couldn't leave it like this. He'd reacted from hurt pride, reacted because he didn't want anyone making decisions for him, forcing his hand. Second guessing what he wanted. He'd been a bastard and he knew it. Lashing out, wanting to hurt her. And the pain he'd barely registered had been real. As real as his. And he knew now why it hurt so much, it was nothing to do with her offer, it was everything to do with the realisation that he'd never see her again. She was somebody else's. She was moving on. Which should have suited him fine.

He took the road back home slowly. Relieved when he pulled in the gateway and there was no sign of life. Parking up the bike he tried to decide what to do. Hassling her now wasn't the way, she needed some space and he had to do it right, even if it damned near killed him. She hadn't bought into a relationship with him, she'd bought in to a bit of fun. And now she'd walked away from it. He absentmindedly checked on the mare, who had a full haynet and no interest in him at all, then with a final check round he went to flick off the barn lights.

Then he saw it. A sheet of paper, shining white in the gloom.

'Jake, I'm sorry for coming back. Sorry for interfering in your life. I promise I won't bother you again. It's between you and Rowena what happens here, like it always should have been. You're right, I can't turn the clock back and I'm not sure I need to any more.

I know I should have told you before, it's yours. Not Sly's. I'm going away, but not with him. Don't worry, I don't want anything from you. I'll be fine G x'

He read it again. Twice. Then ripped it into four pieces and watched as it floated slowly down to the ground.

Then he bent down and collected the pieces and put them back together again. Who the hell did she think she was? Walking in, turning his life upside down and then just waltzing away as though nothing had happened? And did 'it's yours' mean what he thought it did?

Chapter Eleven

"Do you think he hates me?"

"Probably." Ella squished the mint leaves against the edge of the glass, then stopped at the almost animal-like moan of pain that had jumped from Georgie. "Kidding, honestly." She peered over the top of the glass which was en-route to her mouth. "You're serious about him aren't you?" She put the glass down and stared. "You are. Don't even try and deny it. Shit, I never thought…" She turned her concentration back to the mojito for a moment. "Are you sure you're really suited, I mean…"

"No, we're not. And he hates me anyway now."

"You've not heard from him then?"

"Nope." Georgie shook her head and tried not to think about how stupid it had been leaving that silly note. "I'm a dork." She buried her head in her hands, then looked up through her fingers at Ella. "I should have just told him instead of wimping out like that."

"I thought you said he wouldn't listen."

"I could have made him. I mean if I'd sat down and refused to move he would have had to listen." Or he might have just thrown me over his shoulder, then over the gate.

"So what are you going to do about it, now, you know."

"Now I'm not pregnant you mean?"

"Yeah, shouldn't you tell him? Do you want another one?" Ella had drained the tall glass and Georgie had hardly taken a sip of hers. "I think I'll get you one anyway, this is going to be a long night." The other girl winked at her, picked up her own empty glass and headed for the bar.

Georgie leaned back with a sigh. She should have been happy, but she felt strangely empty. Exactly on cue, the day after leaving the note for Jake, her period had started. And although it was good, the best thing that could have happened, she had burst into horrible spontaneous tears and babbling incoherently had rung Ella. Who didn't understand a word, especially as she hadn't even known Georgie had thought she was 'with child' as Ella coyly put it.

And now she wasn't with child, and probably never had been. So much for all the knowing looks from Carol and Rowena.

"Maybe they just thought you looked peaky." Ella dumped the glasses down abruptly on the table, sending a splosh of sugary cocktail onto the table and breaking into her thoughts. "Carol and that other woman, whatever her name is. They might have just thought you looked a bit off and you jumped to conclusions because you were paranoid." She patted Georgie's hand to take the sting of the words away.

Yeah, she'd jumped to conclusions. "But I was so late and I'm never ever late."

"Probably all that extra exercise you've been getting." Ella's tone was dry. "All the bareback riding. Buggered up your body, doesn't know whether it's coming or coming." She giggled at her own joke.

"You're being crude, anyhow now it looks like it's going, going, gone."

"Yup, I am being crude and you're being defeatist. Drink up. We've got evil plans to hatch."

"Maybe I should just leave it."

"Oh no, girl. One, there is no way you can leave him thinking he's gonna be a daddy, and you know it. And two."

"Two?"

"Well if you don't want him you could at least have the decency to introduce him properly to me."

"Ella!"

"Waste not want not, and talking of which drink that mojito before the mint starts growing."

Georgie sipped hard through the straw and let the icy liquid fill her mouth, drift down her throat. "He really doesn't want to get involved with anyone."

"So? When did that make any difference?"

"We're totally unsuited," she took another sip, then decided to ditch the straw, "apart from in the sack."

"And with the horse stuff."

"I suppose."

"And he makes you laugh, and chases off the money grabbing jerks that follow you around. And you go all doe eyed when he's around."

"No, I don't."

"Limp and pathetic?"

"Sod off."

"Soggy with lust?"

"Eurgh. Now you're just been yucky. I admit I fancy him, okay? And the things he does to me…"

"See, you're going limp and pathetic. That's probably why Carol was worried about you. Anyway, does he really know why you wanted to buy the land for him?" Ella's eyes had narrowed to slits, though it didn't stop her slurping up the rest of her mojito.

"Which is?"

"Only you know the full answer to that, honey. Are you drinking that?"

"No, you have it." She pushed the glass over.

"Well at least tell him the reasons why you didn't do it, like you weren't trying to tie him down, although that idea does sound nice."

"Ella."

"And you weren't doing it because you felt sorry for him, or were buying him off, or you'd just got bored of the idea. Just tell him you're a silly cow."

"Thanks for those words of wisdom."

"Well you are. Just tell him you love him." She downed half of Georgie's drink and grinned. "Oh, and don't forget the bit that you're not preggers."

"Who said I," just say the four letter word, you can say it, she swallowed to clear the lump from her throat, "love him?"

"You just did. Shall we go and get a pizza? So, what are you going to do now you know you're not up the duff? I mean you're not really serious about working with your pa are you? You'd hate it, and you don't need the security now."

"God knows, and he's not telling. I screwed up didn't I? But anyhow at least doing that plan did make me think a bit about what I could do. I'm going to look for a place of my own I think, rent something."

"You won't go and work for Alfie though?"

"No." She sighed. "I think I said that partly to please him, because we were having a lovely father daughter thing going, and partly to persuade myself I'd done the right thing running away. If I'm honest," she looked through her eyelashes up at Ella who was sipping at the dregs in the bottom of the glass, "I did want to stay here."

"Well, stay."

The soft words caught her unawares, caught at something deep inside her, she felt like crying, but it wouldn't help. "I can't, he needs this place more than I do. He does Ella, that's why he has to have it. I thought if I used my trust money and bought it for him then it wasn't actually tying him down. He could sell it if he wanted and go, I don't know, wherever. But I think he really wants to be there, whatever he says. Rowena's clever, she knows he needs that place, she was just trying to force him to see it."

"But she was clever enough to know that she couldn't be seen to be forcing him."

"Yeah, and I'm the thick one. She did try and warn me."

"Can you afford to just give it to him, I mean it's a lot of money isn't it? And I thought you were broke."

"When Dad sold it to Rowena he put the money into a trust fund for me, so that if I ever wanted it back…"

"Shit, no kidding? Wow."

"I only found out by accident, he wasn't going to tell me until I'd sorted myself out. It was like a bonus once I'd proved I knew what I wanted and was going to settle down."

"Doesn't he mind you giving it away?"

"He doesn't know. And anyhow Jake doesn't want it, I think I've just got to leave it to him and Rowena to sort out."

"After you've told him."

"Yeah, yeah."

"Look girl, you've got a choice. You can either text him and tell him he it was all a mistake, you're not up the duff and you're sorry for scaring the shit out of him. Or," she fixed Georgie with an assessing glare, "you can admit you messed up, tell him you still fancy him like fuck, and tell him to stop being a wuss and fight you fair and square for that stupid field. Though Christ knows why anyone would be bothered about that." She shook her head, then threw it back and gave a throaty roar that made half the bar turn round and stare. "Oh for fuck's sake, I just got it. Neither of you really give a shit about it do you?"

"You're losing it." Georgie kept her head down and hoped everyone would look away.

"Both of you could just start over somewhere else couldn't you? I mean, yeah I get the old nostalgia thing when you first went back, but you know it's not going to change anything don't you?" She laid a heavy hand on Georgie's knee. "You need a place and a job, but why here?" She didn't stop for an answer, Ella was on a roll. Unstoppable. "And he, he's more pissed off about the fact he thought you were seeing someone else, isn't he? I reckon he would have forgiven you trying to buy the place for him if you'd been staying, but throwing him the scraps before you wandered off with someone better, well that was a real kick in the balls."

"Bollocks." It would have been easier if she'd been drunk. She could have just ignored it then, safe in the knowledge that it would all be forgotten by tomorrow.

"Prove it. You go and ask him."

"Right now?" She picked up her mobile and Ella laughed.

"Face to face, honey. I want to see you face to face."

"No way am I talking to him in front of you."

"You smacked him in the ego and he's smarting, which is why he's not talking to you."

"Neither of us is talking. And he is bothered, he needs that place. Ella, he's been hiding behind the fact of looking after Rowena, but he loves it there. He needs it, it's the only thing he's ever had."

"I thought he didn't want anything, he's a gypsy boy at heart."

"He does need it, he needs something." Or someone.

"Exactly." Ella picked up her jacket. "That boy certainly needs something."

Exactly. What was that supposed to mean?

"Come on, let's go grab that pizza now we've got everything straight."

She could have argued, but it was so much easier not to.

By the time the pizza and another bottle of wine had been polished off Georgie felt like she was caught in the middle of a herd of stampeding elephants. And much as she loved the straight talking Ella she had never been more pleased to see the back of her.

She sank back into the settee and closed her eyes. And never felt less like going to sleep. It was stupid, so totally irrational, but she'd felt like a bit of her had been dragged away when she'd found out she wasn't pregnant. She didn't like babies, didn't want one, but however much she repeated it in her head, or even out loud, there was a loss inside her that was crying out for someone to listen. A silly, useless part of her that wanted to mourn.

She hugged a cushion to herself and stared at the blank TV

screen. And she missed Jake. Ella was right. It was about him now. She scrunched her eyes up. Last time, when her mum had walked she'd had no control, no say over what had happened. This time she could at least try.

And even though she was a little bit tipsy, well maybe because she was, she had to do it now.

She pulled on a worn ripped pair of jeans over her stockings, wrapped a cardigan that had seen better days over the top of the dress she'd worn to go out in, and pushed her feet into old green wellingtons. Pulled a coat from the hook behind the door.

She'd tell him now. Tell him she missed him, tell him she was only trying to help, tell him she knew he hated her, tell him she'd not been with anyone else since that day she'd bumped into him. Tell him she wasn't trying to tie him down or make him stay, well maybe she was a bit, but not really, it was up to him, she liked having him there but she was happy just having fun. Like they had been. She just didn't really want it to end like this. Not yet.

She pushed her cycle over the gravel driveway, trying to be quiet so no-one would hear her from the house. Used a car to balance herself as she set off wobbling down the road. Swearing under her breath as she weaved herself down the dark, narrow lane, nearly falling off every time a branch moved and the moon sent a weird shadow across her path.

The barn was bathed in darkness. No sound apart from the mare occasionally shifting about in her stall, the gentle wicker of welcome she'd sent out when the door opened.

Georgie walked down towards the stall where he kept his motorbike. Empty apart from a half drunk mug of cold coffee. She could go. She should go. She sank down onto one of the bales of hay, slipped from it to sit on the rubber covered floor. If she stayed for just a little while he'd come back, he'd be out drinking, but he'd be back soon. To check on the horse. Oh Lord, what if he had someone with him? She pulled the cardigan tighter around herself, wrapped herself in the old black duffel coat she'd grabbed.

Listened to the hypnotic soft munching of the mare eating hay.

***

Jake studied her for a moment, letting her familiar form, her familiar smell settle inside him before he spoke. "Well, hello stranger. Not got a home to go to?"

She was sat on the floor in the barn, right next to where his bike had been parked earlier. Her knees pulled up, forehead resting on them, and she muttered something which could have been more or less anything ranging from 'I haven't' to 'I hate you'.

"Sorry?" He squatted down in front of her. Close up she looked like a tight ball of stress, tension cloaking her from shoulders to curled-up toes. She muttered again, something indistinct, but when he tapped her arm she finally lifted her head. Long hair sticking to her damp face. "How long have you been here?"

"A while." She rubbed a forearm across her eyes, sniffed. "I went out with Ella. Then I came to see you. I'm allowed aren't I?" She shivered involuntarily and he instinctively moved round to her side. Draped his jacket over her tense shoulders. "Or do you hate me so much you never want to see me again?"

"I don't hate you."

"What time is it?" She stared blearily at him.

"Late."

"Where've you been?"

"Well, strangely enough I went to see you."

"But I wasn't in." She tilted her head on one side, surveyed him through dark eyelashes and a tangle of hair. A whisper from the past that sent an ache of longing deep inside him. He'd wanted that sweet little girl lost a long time ago, and he still wanted her now. Whatever.

He cleared his throat. "Nope, you weren't."

"Why? Why did you go to see me?"

"I'm allowed aren't I? Or do you hate me so much you never

want to see me again?"

She half smiled, relaxed against him. "I don't hate you."

"Loving your get up by the way."

"It's very 'in' this season, wellies and stockings."

"You've got stockings under that get up?"

"Under the jeans I have, yes. You have just got no idea of fashion at all have you?"

He could have throttled her for just turning up when he needed her most, crashing back into his world. But instead he was smiling like some simpleton. "And the duffel coat over the," he lifted a bit of the coat, "moth eaten cardigan over the," rooted a bit further, "satin type thingy."

"It's a dress."

"Thanks. Over the satin dress, that's in this year is it too?"

"Very. Just what the party girl who lives in the cold English countryside needs."

"Is it what you need?"

"Partly." She shuffled about a bit, but didn't go far. "Why were you at my house?"

"I thought maybe it was time we had a chat."

"Ah."

"What's the ahh for?"

"Jake." He felt her take a deep breath. Felt her ease away from him like she was about to say something he didn't want to hear. Forced himself to sit still, listen. "Jake, it was yours. There was no lover boy." She gave another sniff, wiped across her face with the back of her hand.

Ahh. The baby. Except he wasn't sure that was why he'd needed to talk to her, but it was obviously what she wanted. She hadn't missed him, hadn't needed to see him. She was just here to sort out the practicalities. "You said. In the note." He could hear the dry tone, hated himself for it. "Don't worry, I won't abandon you, just tell me how you want to play it."

"Jake, please listen to me."

"I thought I was." Damn, how could he have all his good intentions blown out of the water with one word from her? He'd wanted to talk, needed to talk. But not this conversation.

"It," a long pause, "would have been yours."

Would have been. "You haven't?" Shit. She couldn't have just gone and got rid of it, even if she didn't want a baby. Not the sweet, caring Georgie he thought he knew, she couldn't…

"I didn't want a baby, but I didn't want there not to be one either." She gave a little wail and crumpled against him. "I'm not pregnant." The words were muffled, but he heard them. Through his damp shirt straight to his heart.

"You're not pregnant? You mean there isn't a baby? Were you ever…. Did you…?"

"No." She wailed again, this time louder. Then started to sob, pressing her face harder into his chest. "But I wanted it." She was hiccupping. "I wanted your baby." Shaking.

Jake could feel himself frown as he wrapped his arms round her. So, she didn't want babies, hated the thought of having one, but now was torn to shreds because it turned out she wasn't pregnant? "Shhh." He hugged her closer.

"Everyone thought I was. Carol did, Rowena did. But I wasn't."

He rocked her gently, hardly able to make out the words between the hiccups. "They said that?"

"No." Another wail. "It was just the way they looked at me. And I'm never late, and I was, and I felt funny. I hated brandy and I couldn't drink and I…"

He wanted to say she'd probably got a bug and an over active imagination, and was stressed. But decided against it.

"I hate babies."

"I know. So, this is good? Yeah?"

"No." She thumped his chest. Hard, then pounded on it with the palm of her hands.

"Why?" He tried to keep his voice steady under the battering he was getting. Put his hand over hers to keep it still.

There was a long pause, the odd sniffle. Then she looked up at him, all tear stained with a look of shock on her face. "I don't know." She opened and closed her mouth, relaxed the arm that had been flailing in his direction. "I don't really know."

"So does this mean you're taking my present back?"

She stared a bit longer, then the slightest trace of a grin tugged at her mouth. "It was an unwanted gift." She sounded a bit more normal, pulled back slightly from him. "You said you didn't want it."

Unwanted baby, unwanted gift. Why did people spend all their lives wanting what they couldn't have, and throwing away what they were offered? Then regretting it. He brushed the hair back from her face, tugged at the last lock that had somehow got stuck in the corner of her mouth. "Feel a bit better now?" She nodded. "I didn't think you wanted a baby? And I mean, you definitely don't want one of mine, darling."

Her gaze wavered on his face. "I didn't, I don't. I'd just got used to the idea, and then… it was gone. I don't mean I didn't want yours, I mean I didn't want a baby, but it's not that I want yours, I don't specifically not want yours, I just—"

"I get the drift, maybe now is the time to shut up?"

"Okay."

So she'd jumped to conclusions, thought she was pregnant and never had time to check before she'd careered off on a new path frantically solving a problem that didn't exist. Slowing down, he was fast discovering, wasn't in Georgie's nature. Taking her time, thinking it through, sticking with something was alien. Reacting impulsively and doing what came from the heart was what made her the girl she was. Chaotic. Like some unstable gas.

Which was why Rowena had tried to make her stop and think. To plan, why she'd forced her to stop flitting between wild ideas, why she'd tried to make her work out what she really wanted.

"I missed you, you mad cow."

"That's not very nice."

"Nope, bloody infuriating."

"I mean calling me a mad cow."

"There are worse things to be called." He ran his palm over her silky smooth hair, took in her scent. "I can't just take this place from you though, I'm sorry."

"I know. I get it now."

"Shall I give you a lift home?"

"Can I stay? I just want to be with you, please?"

"In my cold, damp caravan?"

"Wherever. Please."

"And then what?"

"And then I'll tell you why I'm here."

***

She lasted exactly two hours, twenty three minutes and six seconds, by her watch, before she knew she couldn't do it. "Jake?"

"Yes."

"Are you asleep?"

"How can I sleep with you wriggling around like you've sat in an ants nest?"

"I'm not a cold, damp, caravan kind of girl I don't think."

He laughed, a deep down, toe-curling good laugh. "Didn't think so. Even with all those clothes on. Come on Cinders let's get you back to your goose down quilt or whatever it is you're used to. Or I could give you a good sorting and see if that works."

"Can you do both?"

144

Chapter Twelve

"This is good."

"Sorry?" She put the kettle down and glanced over at him. At the crumpled sheets of paper that she thought she'd hidden under the bed. Obviously not, more like down the side of the settee. "Oh, that. Well, it doesn't matter now. Here, coffee."

He ignored the coffee. "No, I mean it. It is, Georgie. You really wanted that place didn't you? You still do."

She shrugged. She had, but it didn't seem quite as important now. "No, I don't. I told you."

"Come on, spill." He held out a large capable hand, she could have ignored it, she could have held on to her coffee mug, but it wouldn't have been fair. Or honest. She put her hand in his, watched his fingers wrap around her much smaller ones. "Sit." She sat, reluctantly. "Now, tell me why you came back."

"For another taste of your body?"

"Georgie." It was stern, a warning. "Okay, let's start with this plan." He tapped the sheets of a paper with one finger. "It's good."

"It's pie in the sky crap."

"No, it's not and you know it, or you're not as smart as I've got you down to be. You've thought it all through, the riding lessons, art centre, shoots, even taking rent off me." The short laugh didn't have any rancour in it. "So, why abandon it now?"

"When I thought—"

"But you're not pregnant, so you can do it."

"When I thought I was, I realised I didn't need this place anymore."

"And you reckoned I did?"

"It's not like that. I know you don't need anything, Jake. But I wanted to give it to you. When Dad came to see me—"

"Did he?" The surprise in Jake's voice was genuine.

"It was the first time we've properly talked for years. I never knew, but my mum hated the whole horse thing you know, she was scared for me. But we did it anyway."

"It isn't why she left, you can't do that old trick of blaming yourself."

"I'm not." And she wasn't. The old Georgie might have, but she'd grown up a bit. "Dad asked me what I wanted and," she paused, "he asked me about you. Jake, I can't turn the clock back, I know I can't, but I can stop myself being like her. I didn't want a baby because kids are where it all goes wrong. Mum had me, and hated the fact that me and dad were so close, then she got pregnant which is why she left—"

"Hey—"

"Can you just let me finish, please? And then Carol got pregnant, and I always felt it was because dad and her had a brood of kids that I was sent away. But it isn't that simple is it? Mum loved me, but it was easier not to be here, and she loved that," what was she supposed to call him? "That, well she loved whoever she ran off with or she wouldn't have gone. And well, I guess Dad needed someone and he met Carol, and I don't think he meant to push me out, I was just a stroppy teenager and he didn't know what to do with me."

"I bet you were. Poor man."

"Thanks for that. And I wouldn't imagine Carol had a clue how to handle things, she's far too nice."

"Not a catty cow?"

"Well, I don't think we're ever going to be best buddies, but she's probably not that bad really." She caught the look he was still shooting her way, "okay, she's not a catty cow. So anyhow," this was the bit where it got more difficult, the bit she'd been turning over and over in her head to try and straighten out the kinks. "Well, I do like it here. I admit it, but it's just…"

"Me?"

"Yes." She glanced up, met that deep sea stare, let herself look at the tumble of dark curls, the dimple in his chin. That perfect, oh so kissable mouth. "Mum and Dad fell for each other, but I guess they shouldn't have got married. She wanted fun, she didn't want kids, didn't want tying down and she wanted it to be just her and Dad. She ran away, and" she risked another look at him, "I don't want to end up doing the same. We're so different, we want different things you and me, and you don't even have a clue what I'm rambling on about do you?"

"I might."

"When I thought I was pregnant, I realised," okay, make a Grade A idiot of yourself, get it over with. "I wanted to be with you, I was making a plan and all the rest because I wanted an excuse to bother you and hang around, but you don't want anything steady, and even if you did, we're just too different and it's just about sex anyway, like it was with—"

She didn't get any further because his mouth was over hers, his tongue running along the tips of her teeth, strong fingers in her hair, against the nape of her neck sending the type of shiver down her spine that she'd been pining for, for days. She groaned and felt the lift at the corner of his mouth.

"Don't laugh at me. I'm—"

He pulled her across the small gap between their chairs, onto his lap. "Bad, you're just so bad." Sharp teeth nipped at her swollen lips just as the warmth of his hand drifted up the inside of her thigh. "Did I tell you how much I like it when all you've got on is a bathrobe?"

"Nope." She squeaked as his teeth moved on to her ear lobe, as his fingers reached the v at the top of her thighs, as they stroked along her swollen labia, gently parted her lips. His fingertips skated lightly over her clit, drifted between her legs then back, circling the swollen nub ever more persistently and she knew she was grabbing at his shoulders, digging her fingers into his hard shoulders. Two fingers slipped deep inside her as this thumb rested against her most sensitive part and the oo mixed with a whimper as she came, an abrupt pulsing, grasping need that she had no control over.

"And now," the dark eyes bored straight into her, "I'm going to put you on that table and fuck you properly."

"You mean, before was just a trail run?"

"Before was nothing, darling."

He lowered her flat on to the large table, pushing her precious plan and the coffee cups until they teetered on the edge, firm thumbs pressing onto the dip just inside her hip bones, holding her still, making her wait. But it wasn't much of a wait, just a brief teeter on the edge before he thrust inside her a slow, unstoppable glide that took him balls deep and her back to the start of a trembling orgasm. She locked her ankles behind the slim hips, held him there as her body trembled around him but could do nothing to control the movement as he tightened his grip around her hips, slid her along the table so that their bodies crashed together with an intensity that made her cry out. She wanted to stop, wanted to control the gentle orgasm that was building inside her, to hold on to it, hold him, feel him, but he wouldn't let her. Each jerk of her body against his made her scared she'd lose it, each thrust deeper made her want more. Then he stopped. She wriggled, trying to move further down the table. He grinned. "Do you want me?" His thumb moved across, pressed against her swollen nub, slowly, painfully circled until she was grasping for breath.

"Yeah." Shit, just do it. His mouth came down, white teeth teased at her nipple sending a new spark all the way down to where his hand pressed against her. The small tremors started, the tremble of a pulse between her legs, she lifted her hips, pressed against him. Cried out as he pulled from her body, a spasm of cold air quickly replaced by the warm dampness of his mouth. She'd had a tongue inside her before, she'd been sucked and teased but this was different. She could feel the strength of his jaw, feel the almost animal need as he lapped and sucked at her, as his tongue flicked deep inside and then he was gently sucking, inescapable, gentle, demanding and she felt like she was bursting under his touch, exploding into his mouth, aware of her thighs trembling against his cheeks, of her hand desperately grasping at his hair.

He flipped her over before she had time to object, to realise what he was doing. The cold wood of the table was against her stomach, her breasts. The heat of his thighs pushing her legs wider and as he pushed inside her still throbbing wet pussy he pressed against her anus, the tip of his finger breaching the tight ring of muscle just enough, just enough to make her clench with anticipation, to tighten around his cock. She was coming again before he did, then the warmth of his explosion bursting inside her kicked off a whole new sensation, and as his warm mouth trailed damp kisses down her neck, her spine, she realised she wanted more.

"Stay." He'd slid her off the table, lifted her up and sunk back onto the settee with her still in his arms,

"I can't stay, Jake. I can't be front of house for ever at the restaurant, and anyway it's starting to get on my nerves. You've no idea what some of the people they get in there are like, and as for the new chef, he thinks he's God's gift—"

He pulled her body tighter against his, hard chin resting on her head. "I mean stay here, with me."

She pulled away, stared at him "With you?" For a second he looked taken aback. "Sorry, that sounds awful, it wasn't supposed to come out like that."

"Would it be such a bad idea? You do your stuff, I do mine. There's room here for both of us."

"But I didn't think—"

"Nor did I." He shrugged self-consciously. "I had a word after you left that note, and Rowena is happy for me to carry on as I am for a bit, until we know if it will work."

"Oh, so you're the one sneaking behind my back now and talking to her."

He laughed. "You'd cut and run, after telling me I was going to be a father. What was I supposed to do?"

"Run after me?"

He laughed again. Louder. "Think about it?"

"We could give it a few weeks. Find out just how compatible we are."

"We could give it in until Valentine's Day…?"

"Jake?"

"Okay, it's a daft idea. All four letter words and yucky romantic stuff as you'd say. Give it until the end of January?"

"Jake, shut up." She pressed her lips against his, fought the urge to close her eyes. "Maybe Carol has a point with her party, and maybe," she took a breath, "maybe all four letter words aren't nasty."

"I quite like some of them actually, like beer, and food, and of course shag."

"We mustn't forget shag. Jake?"

"It makes me scared when you say Jake like that."

"Would it make you scared if I said that I just think, well I, well, the thing is…"

"Oh, Georgina." He was grinning. "I've got a horrible feeling I've fallen for you."

"As in, well, fallen in…"

"As in fallen a long way," there was a crinkle round his eyes, the dimple in his chin had deepened. "All," he kissed her nose, "the way."

www.ingramcontent.com/pod-product-compliance
Lightning Source LLC
Chambersburg PA
CBHW010858130726
47900CB00017B/2921